Amy Cross is the author of more than 200 horror, paranormal, fantasy and thriller novels.

THE HAUNTING OF STRYKE BROTHERS

THE GHOSTS OF CROWFORD BOOK 17

AMY CROSS

This edition
first published by Blackwych Books Ltd
United Kingdom, 2024

Also available in e-book format.

www.amycross.com
www.blackwychbooks.com

CONTENTS

THE
HAUNTING
OF
STRYKE
BROTHERS

PROLOGUE ONE

1949...

"YOUNG LADY, LET ME be the first to introduce you to the future. I don't know if you've ever set foot in our marvelous establishment before, but you're in for a treat. Welcome to Stryke Brothers!"

Stopping near the jewelry desk, Walter Stryke turned and held his arms out as if to emphasize the vast size of the shop floor.

"You won't find a better department store in this part of Kent," he continued, clearly warming to his theme. "Hell, I don't think you'll find a better department store this side of the Medway. My brother and I have been building this place up since before the war, and I think we're really on the verge of turning it into something tremendous. And now you, my dear, have a chance to become part of the story. What do you think?"

"Well," Dorothy Maitland said, somewhat taken aback by his brashness, "it seems very... nice."

"Nice?"

"Lovely, in fact."

"Dorothy," he replied, shaking his head sadly as he walked back over and put an arm around her shoulders, "Stryke Brothers isn't here to be nice, and it's certainly not here to be lovely." He pointed over at the far side of the shop. "Glassware," he continued. "Tableware. Linen. Cutlery. Kitchen equipment that any wife in the country would kill for. Wool. Can you believe that we sell wool? Little figurines and other decorations. Dollies for the little girls, toy soldiers for the little boys." He pointed toward the rear. "Cushions. Blankets. Pillows and other bedding." He pointed at the other side. "Vases. Cups. Ceramic bits and bobs. Trinkets galore. Pictures in frames that you can stick on your walls."

He pointed at the stairs.

"And that's just on this floor," he added.

"Including the basement, we have four floors covering just about any kind of item a person could want, all right here in sunny little Crowford. We've even got a toy section for the very youngest babies. Unless it's edible, there's nothing you can't buy right here at Stryke Brothers. I've thought of everything, and if there's something I *haven't* thought of, then I'll find a way to squeeze it in with everything else. There's always another little corner where I can fit an extra shelf or a new display. This, my dear, is the future of shopping!"

"It's very impressive," she admitted, although there was still a trace of caution in her voice. "I've really never seen anything like it."

"And this isn't even its final form," he continued, with his arm still wrapped round her. "We're constantly developing, constantly innovating, constantly looking for new opportunities. That's my particular area of genius, I've always been good at predicting the future. Show me a housewife and I'll tell you not only what she wants now, but also what she's gonna want in five years from now, and ten years, and even twenty. Tell me, Dorothy, are you married?"

"I'm not, no."

"I see," he replied, conspicuously looking

her up and down. "You'll make a fine wife for someone."

"Thank you," she said, trying not to blush.

"And if you're lucky, your fella'll bring you here to do some shopping," he continued. "Tell me, Dorothy, do you have a fella at the moment?"

"I don't, no."

"A pretty young thing like you?" he said, once again looking her up and down. "I find that hard to believe, Dorothy. How old are you, again?"

"I'm twenty-one, Mr. Stryke."

"A fine age," he muttered, staring at her chest. "A very fine age indeed. You've got a lot to learn, Dorothy, but that's where I come in. I need pretty young things such as yourself to work on my counters. When you walked through that door, I immediately knew that I wanted to hire you. I've always liked hiring women to work for me, even before it was fashionable. And I can tell that you and I are going to go to great places together."

"I'm quite happy with just a little job," she demurred. "Just something to... tide myself over while my father can't work. He got injured in the pit, and he gets a little money but I want to chip in and help Mum out where I can. You understand, don't you?"

"Implicitly and explicitly," he told her, still watching her chest. "You know, Dorothy, I've got a very good feeling about you. I think you might be exactly the type of girl I've been waiting for!"

***

"One hundred years from now," Walter continued as he led her up to the very top floor, where assorted fur coats were on display, "do you know what people are going to be saying? They're going to be saying that shopping is an art-form, and they're going to be saying that Walter Stryke was the Van Gogh or Da Vinci of the medium."

"I'm sure," Dorothy replied, reaching the top of the stairs and looking around at the hats on various stands. "Mr. Stryke, the advertisement didn't mention -"

"And you get to play a vital part in the story," he said, interrupting her as he took one of the hats and carried it over, placing it on her head. "Don't you find that exciting?"

"Absolutely," she replied, removing the hat and setting it aside as he took a fur coat from a mannequin. "Mr. Stryke, I hate to ask about the financial side of things, but pay is -"

"Try this on," he said, holding the fur coat up.

"I'm not sure that -"

"Just try it on!" he insisted, stepping around behind her and forcibly wrapping the coat over her shoulders. "There!" he added, taking a step back to admire her. "Ms. Maitland, you look positively divine! If I ever get around to producing an advertisement for my products, you simply must do some modeling for me. Have you posed for artistic purposes before?"

"No," she replied, "and -"

"You're a natural," he continued, making his way around her, taking care to admire her from head to toe. "There are some extra perks to this job, you know. If you work for me, you can sometimes borrow items from the store. Why, in some cases you can even keep them."

"That's lovely, but -"

"I like my employees to look good," he told her. "They're part of the Stryke Brothers brand. Do you know much about brands, Ms. Maitland?"

"I do not."

"Well, I'm a veritable pioneer," he explained as he stopped in front of her. "You're a very pretty young thing, and I think you have potential to go far. It's not like the days before the war, when women were expected to remain in the home at all times, only venturing out on the arms of young gentlemen. One might even say that we're entering a world designed specifically for women, one where there are no barriers between the sexes. Does that idea excite you, Ms. Maitland?"

"I just want a job so that I can contribute at home," she explained meekly. "Mum scrimps and saves, and with Dad off sick there's just not so much to go round. Even a small amount would let me help out. Dad doesn't like that thought, but he doesn't really have a say in the matter, not until his back heals."

"Indeed," Walter purred, still keeping his eyes fixed on her. "Well, the good news is that you've got the job."

"I have?" she replied, shocked by the sudden news.

"You had it from the moment you stepped through the door downstairs," he told her. "One day you're going to look back on this moment as the start of something very exciting. Why, I truly believe that eventually you could even take over the entire store and run it yourself! You might one day be sitting in my office, behind my desk, hiring and firing people just the way that I do. Doesn't the whole idea sound absolutely wonderful?"

"Oh, I don't think that I'd be very good at that," she demurred. "I'm really not sure that I'm cut out for so much pressure."

"I shall take you under my wing and teach you everything that I know," he promised, before pausing for a moment. "The whole world is your oyster, Ms. Maitland. Might I call you Dorothy?"

"Of course," she replied, although she felt sure he'd already been doing so.

"The whole world is your oyster, Dorothy," he continued, fixing her with a determined stare that made her feel distinctly uncomfortable. A moment later he reached over and took hold of her hand, squeezing it gently before placing his other hand on her waist. "I'm giving you something wonderful," he added with a smile. "Something that no other man in all of Crowford can give you. The question now becomes... what are you going to give me in return?"

PROLOGUE TWO

2013...

"I'M BORED," CHRIS SAID, sitting on a bench in Crowford High Street, swinging his legs aimlessly as he looked around at the various shuttered shops. "There's nothing to do here."

"Tell me about it," Craig muttered, slumped next to him, watching as an elderly woman pulled a shopping cart into one of the alleys. "This town's completely dead. Even my mum's stopped arguing that there's any hope round here. We're moving as soon as they've finalized selling our house to the army."

"Same," Chris said with a heavy sigh. "I don't get why the army want to buy the whole town, but I don't think anyone can stop them now. It's not even like there's anywhere left to go here, anyway. Most of the shops are shut, and most of the pubs too."

"Give it six months and Crowford'll be a ghost town," Craig replied. "Everyone knows it's true. Then the army can do what they want with it. They can run around pretending to be at war, and there'll be no-one left to care. Mum says the library's going to shut soon."

He paused for a moment, looking along the street, before sighing heavily as he hauled himself up.

"Even the seagulls don't bother coming round," he pointed out. "Come on, I'm sick of sitting here looking at all the empty buildings." He turned and looked at a couple of old shops nearby, which had long since been boarded up and left to rot. "My dad told me that used to be a coffee shop," he continued, "and that one next to it was a shoe shop. Now look at them. They're both empty."

He looked all around.

"Everything's empty. The whole town's gone to the dogs."

"Where are we going, then?" Chris asked, standing up and kicking a stone, sending it skittering across the ground. "Don't say the seafront again, because -"

Before he could finish, they both heard the sound of a phone ringing. They turned and looked at the nearby public phone, which was suddenly ringing after staying quiet for so many years. After glancing at one another, the boys hesitated for a moment longer until finally Chris stepped forward. Reaching out, Craig grabbed his arm.

"Don't answer it," he said firmly.

"Why not?" Chris asked.

"Haven't you heard the stories? That phone's haunted."

"The phone?" Chris replied skeptically. "Are you crazy?"

"No, it's true, my nan told me!" Craig exclaimed. "You know how there are, like, a million ghost stories about Crowford? She used to tell me some of them, and one time she told me everyone knows that phone is haunted."

"It's just ringing, that's all," Chris said.

"Yeah, but look at the cord."

Chris opened his mouth to reply, to tell his friend that he was crazy, but at the last second he saw that the cord was broken, meaning that the receiver wasn't actually connected to the phone itself. He swallowed hard, before reminding himself that the ringing section was in the main body, so the separated receiver didn't actually mean anything. To prove that point, he bolted forward and grabbed the receiver.

"Don't!" Craig hissed.

"Hello?" Chris said, grinning from ear to ear. "Anyone there? Any ghosts?"

He waited, but after a moment the grin began to fade from his lips. After a moment longer, he set the receiver down and took a step back.

"What is it?" Craig asked. "Did you hear something?"

"I'm not sure," Chris replied, looking a little pale as he turned to him. "I think... I don't know, but I might have done. Like a voice, whispering really quietly, asking for help."

"Don't be stupid," Craig replied, offering a slightly unconvincing smile. "You won't fool me, you know."

"I'm telling the truth!" Chris said firmly. "If you don't believe me, listen for yourself."

"Boys?" a voice called out, and they turned to see Craig's mother Marilyn waving at them from the far corner. "Come on, I've been looking for you everywhere! We've got to get home and start packing. Chris, you can come too if you like. Do you want me to make some dinner for you?"

"Let's go," Craig muttered, grabbing Chris by the arm and pulling him along the street. "I'm sick of hanging around like I've got nothing better to do."

"You don't think that phone was actually haunted, do you?" Chris replied, glancing back at the payphone. "I heard something, but I suppose it could have just been the wind or a crossed connection or something."

"Of course it's not haunted," Craig said as they made their way around the corner. "Think about it, you idiot. What kind of ghost would haunt a phone?"

Once they were gone, Crowford High Street stood still and empty. A breeze blew some leaves along the ground and gently rocked a damaged bin, but otherwise there was no sign of movement. The payphone stood in its usual place outside the shuttered coffee shop, with the loose receiver resting on the top. No-one was around to listen, but if they had been, they might have picked the receiver up and listened carefully; and if they'd waited a few seconds, they too might have heard the faintest whispered cry for help.

CHAPTER ONE

1998...

"OKAY, THANKS A LOT," Josh said, reaching out to steady the metal cage as its wheels squeaked against the tiled floor. "Same time next week?"

The delivery man offered only a grunt in reply, before turning and stomping his way out to the lorry that he'd parked in the street.

"Same time next week," Josh said with a smile, heading to the door and swinging it shut, then reaching up to slide the bolt into place. "It was lovely to see you again, Patrick," he continued. "These little interactions of ours really are a highlight of my social calendar each week. Of course, it helps that you're such a cheery figure, full of optimism about life."

Patrick stopped for a moment, reaching into the back of his trousers to scratch some part of his body that Josh preferred not to think about too much.

"Great, Patrick," he added under his breath. "Go easy now. See you again next week."

He watched as Patrick climbed back into the lorry. Wednesday nights were always delivery nights at Al's Coffee, at least when the owner wasn't locked into another non-payment dispute with the wholesaler. Having worked at Al's for a couple of years now, and as the last remaining full-time employee, Josh had learned to swing with the punches and accept all the chaos. In truth, he didn't even mind staying late on Wednesdays, even though the delivery lorry often failed to appear until close to midnight. And as the lorry drove away now, past the smattering of shops and boarded-up former shops on the High Street, Josh reminded himself that he'd miss the routine when it was gone.

Which, judging by the lack of customers recently, wouldn't take much longer.

Turning to the cage, he began to wheel it

past the chairs and over toward the counter. As he did so, however, he spotted something moving at the far end, over by the door to the toilets. Stopping, he peered into the darkness, but now he saw only shadows. A moment later he heard a shuffling sound, and he began to worry that somehow one of the customers might have ended up locked in the toilet earlier when the shop was closed.

"Hello?" he called out. "Is anyone there?"

Hearing no reply, he pushed the cage all the way to the door that led into the storage room, and then he wandered to the toilet door. He listened for a moment before pulling the door open and peering into the bathroom, but all he saw was the toilet and the washbasin, and he realized now that no-one could possibly have ended up trapped in there, since he'd already cleaned this part of the shop.

Suddenly something bumped against the metal cage, and Josh turned to look back across the shop. Most of the lights were off, but a few had been left on near the counter, and Josh couldn't help but wonder whether he might have company after all. The shop could be a rather spooky place late at night sometimes, even if the chiller cabinets and racks of promotional coffee bags weren't entirely conducive to a ghostly atmosphere.

"Hello?" he said again, walking back around the counter to make sure that no local kids had crept in to play a prank. Spotting nobody, he listened for a moment longer. "If there's anyone here, you might as well come out now. I don't get paid enough to deal with kids, and I *definitely* don't get paid enough to be haunted."

He waited, and a moment later he heard a distinctive knocking sound on the wall. He turned to look at the spot directly above the sink, and sure enough the knocking sound continued. This time, however, Josh knew exactly what was happening, and a smile crossed his face as he realized that his favorite person in the whole world was on the other side of that wall.

***

"I hate these late nights," Sasha said, sitting next to Josh on the shared metal steps that served as the rear fire escape for both Al's Coffee and next door's Stanley's Shoes. "Why can't delivery people come during the day?"

She took a drag on her cigarette.

"Don't answer that," she added, sounding even more bored than usual. "I know the answer. It just sucks ass, that's all."

For a moment, not really knowing what to say, Josh simply looked out at the marvelous view. From their spot perched on the fire escape, he and Sasha could see all the way across the rear car park of Benson's Supermarket; the parking bays were empty so close to midnight, of course, but some old trolleys had been left in various spots, waiting to be gathered up in the morning, and a solitary security light picked out the supermarket's rear delivery door. Josh opened his mouth to suggest that the view was strangely beautiful, in a rundown urban kind of way, but at the last moment he reminded himself that Sasha tended to not be quite so sentimental.

"Yeah," he managed finally, once again feeling tongue-tied around such a beautiful girl. "It totally sucks ass."

"What's up with you, anyway?" she asked. "I saw the lorry just now, your delivery's been already. Why aren't you putting it all away and heading home?"

"There's no rush."

"There's totally a rush," she reminded him. "Does Al pay you to stay behind for the deliveries?"

"No, but -"

"So why are you still here, man?" she continued incredulously. "What could possibly keep you behind so late?"

He opened his mouth to reply, but for a few seconds he was struck by her beauty in the moonlight. Worried that he was staring, he turned and looking across the car park.

"I hate my job," Sasha said after a few seconds, "and I hate my life, and I hate this town, and I just want to get the hell out of here as fast as I can."

"Where do you want to go?" he asked.

"Literally anywhere," she said, rolling her eyes. "Crowford's dying, man. Give it another decade and there'll be no-one left."

"You don't know that," he replied. "I know things seem kind of dead now, but these things always go in cycles. We've got the new millennium coming up, and that's going to bring a whole load of change. Crowford's been through bad patches and downturns before, at least according to my nan. I bet within a couple of years you'll start to see things getting better again."

"Nope," she said, taking another drag on her cigarette. "This is it. This is the death spiral. There's not going to be any grand resurgence. The town isn't going to miraculously rise again like a phoenix from the ashes. This time it's terminal, and they might as well pave over the entire place and call it a day." She examined the end of her cigarette for a moment. "Of course, by then I plan to be long gone. You should be too. I mean, you don't seriously want to be managing a crumby little coffee shop for the rest of your life, do you?"

"No!" he protested.

"What do you want to do? What's your ambition?"

"Well, I haven't quite figured that out yet," he told her. "I mean, there are lots of things I *could* do. The world's a big place and there aren't really any limits, but I've got loads of ideas." He tried to think of a few, of at least one he could mention to try to impress her, but already he knew that he was sounding pretty bad. "I've been thinking of applying to college in Canterbury," he added after a moment. "They do lots of great courses and I could get there by bus and still work part-time here at Al's, and I'd save money by living with my gran and then after a few years I should be in a great position. After finishing school last year I kind of wanted to earn some money first, but now I'm feeling like I'm raring to go."

"Huh," she replied, "well, that sounds... very sensible."

"Thanks," he said with a smile, before suddenly worrying that this was a bad thing and that she'd been making fun of him. "Wait, is -"

In that instant, a loud bump rang out from inside the shoe shop, accompanied by a clattering sound. Josh and Sasha both turned to look back into the office beyond the fire escape, and after a moment Sasha stubbed out her cigarette before getting to her feet.

"It's her!" she exclaimed.

"Who?" Josh asked.

"Don't you know anything about this town?" she asked with a sigh, before hurrying back inside. "The shoe shop's totally haunted! She doesn't come out every night, but she's definitely here right now! Come on, if we're lucky we might even get to see her!"

"Haunted?" he replied, sounding somewhat confused as he hauled himself up. "The shoe shop? A haunted shoe shop? Sorry, but... why would a ghost ever want to haunt a shoe shop?"

CHAPTER TWO

"STAY QUIET," SASHA WHISPERED, stepping onto the shoe shop's sales floor and looking across the darkened space. "Don't scare her off."

"Scare who off?" Josh asked, following a few paces behind and stopping next to a rack of discounted trainers. "Oh, you mean the ghost?"

"I've never really seen her properly," Sasha continued, keeping her voice low. "Just hints, really, and occasionally a muffled cry. Believe me, it took me a hell of a long time to believe that this thing could be real. I mean, ghosts are supposed to haunt mansions and castles and places that are a bit more grand, but this particular ghost seems determined to haunt the shoe shop."

"We have one next door," Josh told her.

She turned to him.

"In the coffee shop?" she asked.

He nodded.

"That's even worse than having one in a shoe shop," she suggested. "If I was a ghost, I'd have much higher standards. I'd refuse to haunt anywhere less than a hundred years old, and I'd damn well want to scare as many people as possible. What does she do in the coffee shop, anyway? Does she rattle the mugs? Does she sort through the beans and rip the teabags open when you're not looking?"

"Nothing quite like that," he said with a smile. "I think she just sort of... hangs out there."

"That's so lame," Sasha told him. "If I -"

Before she could finish, they both heard a bumping sound nearby. Turning, they saw that one of the temporary displays was shaking slightly, as if it had recently been knocked.

"Okay," Josh said, feeling a growing sense of dread, "I have to admit, *that's* kind of freaky. You don't have mice or rats in here, do you?"

Sasha opened her mouth to reply, but hearing a scuffing sound over by the wall. She looked at the spot where various posters had been left up, and she realized after a few seconds that she was holding her breath as she waited for the ghostly presence to make its reappearance.

"It's like it was walking that way," she pointed out finally. "Why would she want to go over there?"

"Beats me," Josh admitted. "It's not really so scary, though, I mean, if she only bumps displays and stuff, what is there to even be scared about?"

"What is there to be scared about?" she asked, turning to him with a shocked expression on her face. "Are you serious? A dead soul returns to this world, haunting the place where she probably died, and you don't think that's in any way remarkable?"

"I guess it's the remaindered trainers that are putting me off," he suggested, looking at a nearby rack. "I'm sorry, but it's a little hard to take a ghost story seriously when it's set in a place like this." He turned and saw a large sign promoting an offer. "Then again, maybe I just don't have enough of an imagination. Not everything can be all about shadows and spooky lighting and cobwebs." He turned to see that Sasha was staring at the wall. "Sorry," he added, "am I boring you?"

"What's on the other side of this?" she asked, placing her hands on the wall. "It's the coffee shop, isn't it?"

"That should be about where the comfy

seats are," he told her. "They're a bit low for some people, but if you ask me -"

"She went through this wall," Sasha continued, interrupting him. "Do you realize what that means?"

***

"She's haunting both places at once," she explained a few minutes later, as she and Josh made their way into the darkened coffee shop. "The ghost of the shoe shop is the same ghost as the ghost of the coffee shop."

"How do you make that out?" he asked.

"Simple." Flicking a switch on the wall, she turned the lights on and looked over at the seats. "That wall wouldn't even have been there when she died. Assuming she died a while ago, at least. Don't you know anything about the history of these buildings?"

"I must have missed that part."

"This was originally Stryke Brothers," she told him. "These two shops would have been the entrance area to that old department store that shut down in the eighties. Someone literally stuck a wall in and divided the whole place down the middle." She made her way to the chairs and looked at them for a moment, before turning to Josh again. "That's great for us, it means two shops instead of one, but as far as the ghost is concerned the new layout is just an inconvenience. That's if she even notices it at all!"

"Okay, fine," he replied, "so there's a ghost haunting the two least spooky places in all of Crowford. Does that matter?"

"She wouldn't be haunting it for no reason, would she?" she pointed out. "You and I both have to stay behind some nights for deliveries, right?"

"Right."

"And on other nights, the shops are shut. They both shut around five."

"Yes, but -"

"So this ghost spends the nights wandering between the two shops," she explained. "There has to be a reason for that. She obviously wants something, and it must be something she can't get for herself."

"How do you know?"

"Because she'd have it by now," she reminded him. "You're really new to all this stuff, aren't you? She must be haunting the shops because she's trying to resolve something that's keeping her spirit here. Ghosts don't *want* to haunt places, they end up trapped here because some part of their life –

or their death – won't let them leave. This ghost wants something and she's trapped in some kind of hellish nightmare until she can get it. Doesn't that horrify you? Doesn't it make you want to find some way to help her?"

"Um..."

Josh thought about that question for a moment, but he quickly realized that this might at least provide an excuse to spend a little more time with the girl of his dreams.

"Totally," he said finally. "You've hit the nail on the head."

"I don't know why I only put two and two together tonight," she continued, making her way back over to him and switching the lights back off, then turning to look across the shop again. "Do you realize what this means? For once, our boring lives might actually have some meaning. Obviously there was some kind of tragedy at the department store, and now the ghost of some dead person – for some reason I'm convinced it's a woman – is haunting the place and seeking redress or revenge or... something else. And it's our job to help her move on to a more peaceful place."

"How are we going to do that?" he asked.

"By delving into the past," she told him. "By being inquisitive. By having some gumption."

She looked at him, and after a few seconds she surprised him by shoving him hard in the chest. "Are you kidding me?" she asked. "Why do I have to spell all of this out to you? Do you not see the attraction of this massive mystery?"

"Sure," he said cautiously, although he immediately realized that he sounded massively underwhelmed. "I'm up for anything, it's just a matter of knowing where to start. I'm sure we've both heard tons of ghost stories about Crowford over the years, sometimes I think we must be living in just about the most haunted place in the entire country. Maybe even the world! Don't you think someone would have noticed this particular ghost before?"

"Someone did," she replied, clearly not impressed by his attitude. "Me!"

"Yes, but I mean someone..." His voice trailed off as he tried to work out exactly how he was going to finish that sentence.

"Important?" she suggested, raising a skeptical eyebrow. "Smart? Useful? Interesting?"

"No, I just meant -"

"Forget it," she replied, turning and heading out of the coffee shop, while raising a single finger to show him exactly what she thought of him. "It's not like I need your help! Have fun stacking bags of coffee on the shelves. That's a really interesting and fulfilling life you've got ahead of you!"

"I didn't mean it like that!" he called after her, before sighing as he realized that he'd completely screwed up and that she probably wouldn't ever want to talk to him again. "Damn it," he muttered, leaning against the counter and putting his hands over his face for a moment. "Well, that's the end of that," he added, dragging his hands down as he stared at the opposite wall. "Back to being a hopeless idiot who has no idea how to talk to girls."

CHAPTER THREE

THREE WEEKS LATER, AS he stepped off the bus and began to make his way along Crowford's main street, Josh couldn't shake a nagging sense of disappointment. He was on his way to another Wednesday evening shift at Al's, and as usual he was going to have to stay late to wait for the delivery lorry, but this wasn't the reason for his disappointment; the reason was that he'd just told Al that he was sticking around at least until Christmas, which meant that any hope of starting college was going to have to wait another year.

And then, as he reached the coffee shop, he saw a series of new posters in the window of the shoe shop next door. Stopping, he stared at the posters as he realized that not only were they advertising a massive sale, they were also plastered with the same two words over and over again. Looking up, he saw more posters in the upstairs windows, directly below the faded old Stryke Brothers frontage that stretched across both shops.

"Closing down," he whispered, reading the posters. After a moment he tilted his head slightly. "Closing down?"

***

"Closing down," Sasha said as she counted some change at the coffee shop's counter and then handed it over to him. "Yeah, we only found out yesterday. Apparently the guys at head office are shutting any branch that makes a loss."

"That place makes a loss?"

"It hasn't turned a profit in five years," she told him, watching as he dropped the coins into the till. "They'd have shut a long time ago, but the lease was still running so I guess they figured they might as well try to get some customers. So much for things only being able to get better, huh? This economy sucks."

"So when do you lose your job?" he asked.

"End of the month."

"Any idea what you'll do next?"

She shrugged, before heading toward the end of the counter so she could wait for her drink.

"Hold on," Josh told the next customer in the line, before grabbing a takeaway cup and heading to the machine so that he could make Sasha's coffee himself. "So," he continued, hoping to keep the conversation going, "I know things haven't exactly been easy between us lately."

"What are you talking about?" she asked, clearly unimpressed.

"Any luck with the ghost hunting?"

"You were probably right, I'm sure no ghost would ever bother to haunt a rundown commercially unsuccessful shoe franchise store." She rolled her eyes. "Sometimes I feel like *I'm* the only one haunting that place. Which I will be soon, because everyone else is already getting jobs at other places in town, so it looks like I'll be managing the shutdown of the entire place."

"I knocked on the wall a few times."

"Yeah, I heard," she said awkwardly, "but... I've been too busy to hang out on the fire escape."

"I was worried you hated me."

"Hatred would imply emotion," she replied, "which would imply giving a damn, which would imply that I'm capable of basic human feelings. Which, at this point in my life, I'm not." She paused as she watched him pouring her coffee. "Besides, sitting on the fire escape with you was fun, but it was also kind of depressing staring out at that car park. Call me crazy, but the back of the supermarket isn't exactly a rich and inspiring view."

"I always enjoyed it," he said eagerly. "I mean... it was almost like a movie scene."

"What movie?" she asked point-blank.

"I don't know."

"Is my coffee ready?"

"Hang on." He headed to the hot water machine and topped the cup up, before making his way to the end of the counter and setting her drink down. "Do you want to go out there again one Wednesday night, while we still have a chance?" he continued. "I don't know, it might feel kind of nostalgic."

"You're weird," she told him. "I don't normally mind weird, but there's a limit and you're pushing it." She picked up her cup and turned to walk away, before hesitating. "By the way," she added, "I'm going to make one last attempt to get proof that there's a ghost in there, before I leave. If I succeed, you'll be the first to know. Hell, I'll shove that stuff in your face like there's no tomorrow. And then I'll probably blow this town forever."

"Do you need some help?" he asked. "With

the ghost thing, I mean."

She opened her mouth to reply, before hesitating for a moment.

"Nah, you're good," she said finally. "I mean, it's not like any of it matters, anyway. And I'm sure the ghost won't appear to me, because let's face it, I'm not important."

"I didn't mean that last time," he said with a sigh, but she was already walking away and he saw that the line at the counter was getting longer. "Sasha?" he called out, even as she made her way outside. "I didn't mean it like that. You're really important." He watched as she disappeared past the window. "And special. And cool. And beautiful."

"Hey," a guy at the front of the line said after a moment, "any chance of getting some coffee?"

***

Several hours later, having closed the shop and taken in the delivery, Josh stopped at the counter and pondered his options. All evening his head had been swirling with the news of the shoe shop's imminent closure, and he couldn't shake the fear that soon Sasha was going to go away and he might never see her again.

"They'd have shut a long time ago," he heard her voice saying in his thoughts, "but the lease was still running so I guess they figured they might as well try to get some customers. I'll probably blow this town forever."

Realizing that she was almost certainly still in the shop next door, waiting for her own delivery, he made his way past the end of the counter and over to the wall. He hesitated for a moment, worried that he might be making a mistake, and then he knocked on the wall; so many times in the past, she'd knocked back to signal that she'd meet him on the fire escape, but deep down he knew that those days were over. Sure enough, as the seconds passed, he heard nothing in reply and he supposed that she was far too busy to bother hanging out with him.

Hearing a scuffing sound, he looked over his shoulder. Most of the shop floor was dark, but he felt sure that he'd heard someone walking past. He waited, briefly wondering whether he might have heard the ghost, before telling himself that he was just wasting time. There clearly wasn't a ghost in the coffee shop, and if there was, it was hardly the most terrifying thing in the world.

He looked at the wall again.

"Okay," he muttered, even though he knew that Sasha wouldn't be able to hear him, "I get it.

Sorry again for being such an idiot a few weeks ago. Good luck with whatever you end up doing next in life."

Again he waited, just in case some kind of miracle might occur, before heading to the door. He switched off the last of the lights, and then once he was outside he locked the shop up ready for reopening in the morning. Taking a few steps back, he looked at the shoe shop next door; a few of the lights were on, but he could see no sign of Sasha and he figured she was probably busy going through the stock upstairs and figuring out what to put out in the final sale. Part of him wanted to knock on the door and offer to help, but he couldn't shake the fear that he might start giving off creepy vibes, and he sighed as he realized that he had to simply leave her alone. He still wished that he'd managed to sweep her off her feet, but that chance had well and truly passed.

Setting off along the street, he made his way past the broken old phone box and the various benches, before reaching the traffic lights and looking both ways. At almost midnight, there was no traffic around at all, and after a moment he glanced over his shoulder. Crowford High Street looked so gloomy and bare, with around half the shops having closed their doors in the previous year.

The town was dying, that much was certain, but worse still he felt as if he and all the other residents were dying with it; he knew he should try to get away, but somehow he felt tied to the place.

Trying to put all those thoughts out of his mind, he headed along the street, making his way toward the train station and then over the bridge, setting off on his long walk home.

CHAPTER FOUR

"CAN A TILL SUPERVISOR please report to the checkout desk?" a Scottish voice asked over the supermarket's fuzzy old speaker system. "Till supervisor to checkout. Thank you."

"Do you know those movies where the guy makes some big romantic gesture and the girl falls for him?" Josh said, standing in the cereal aisle and watching as Tommo added more boxes to the shelves. "Are those movies just completely made up? Does stuff like that *ever* work in the real world?"

"Not that I've ever seen," Tommo replied, kneeling to sort the boxes on the shelf at the bottom. "Man, you've got it bad, haven't you? I've never heard you talking about a girl like this before."

"I just think she's really special, that's all,"

he admitted. "We've talked loads over the years, and we have so much in common."

"Such as?"

"We like some of the same music."

"Not enough. Next?"

"We like some of the same films."

"Again, not enough to serve as the foundation of a healthy relationship. Next?"

"She goes to Nelson's sometimes," he pointed out. "I go there too."

"You're really reaching here."

"We're both into ghosts," he added. "We have this running theory that the shoe shop and the coffee shop are haunted by the same ghost."

Tommo looked up at him with a skeptical expression on his face.

"It's because they used to be one shop," Josh continued. "Stryke Brothers was this department store until, like, the eighties. Apparently it was the height of glamour."

"Alright, Peter Venkman," Tommo replied, "that's great, but it's still not enough to get the girl to like you. Have you even seen this ghost, anyway?"

"No," Josh replied. "To be honest, it's kind of hard to take it seriously. Ghosts haunt spooky old houses and churches, and cemeteries, and abandoned houses. Not well-lit coffee shops and random places in the middle of a rundown town."

"Help me up," Tommo said, reaching out so that Josh could support him. Letting out a gasp, he hauled himself to his feet. "I'm twenty-one years old," he continued, "and my knees are shot from working in this hellhole. Do you know what I'm haunted by? The ghost of my own potential."

"Do you ever think about quitting?"

"And working where?" Tommo asked. "At least Benson's is going to be around for a long time. Hang on, I need to go and get another pallet of Puffy Puff Puffs."

"That's not a real cereal," Josh replied as Tommo smirked and walked off. "Is it? Is there actually a cereal brand called Puffy Puff Puffs?"

Left alone in the aisle, he turned and watched as an elderly woman slowly pushed her trolley past. The woman looked up at him with sad, slightly milky eyes, and Josh offered a smile as she made her way closer; she merely stared back at him with no real expression, struggling as the trolley's wayward wheels tried to pull her in different directions and then she headed over to the shelf with all the coffee and tea. Watching her trembling hand reaching out for a box of tea bags, Josh realized that she'd probably lived her entire life in Crowford, and he supposed that he too was probably going to be just like that.

At least Sasha had plans to get out. Deep down, he felt sure that he was never even going to get as far as the college in Canterbury.

After a couple of minutes, with Tommo still having not returned, Josh checked his watch and considered leaving. He had a rare day off from the coffee shop, and he needed to pick up some things in the town for his grandmother before going home and watching some videos, then heading out to see a band; he also needed to pop into the library and use their computer, since it was – as far as he knew – the only machine in the entire town connected to the internet, and he wanted to research some old eighties television shows he only dimly remembered.

Glancing along the brightly-lit aisle, he spotted a man slowly making his way around the corner, and in that moment he froze as he realized that there was something a little strange about this guy.

Walking slowly and stiffly, the man was wearing slightly old-fashioned dark clothing, a kind of suit complete with a showy handkerchief in one pocket. The suit was strange enough, like something from one of the town's many charity shops, but Josh was particularly struck by the man's features; he looked extremely pale, and his eyes were dark and shadowy, with deep rings underneath. Although he told himself that he was imagining things, Josh couldn't shake the sense that this man looked like a member of the walking dead, and he felt a shiver run through his bones as the man turned and glared straight at him.

Offering a faint, somewhat forced smile, Josh immediately noted that this effort was in no way reciprocated. In fact, the man's eyes seemed angrier now, as Josh felt more and more certain that he was staring into the face of a dead soul.

"Here!" Tommo said suddenly, shoving a box at him from behind. "Puffy Puff Puffs."

Startled, Josh turned to him and saw the box. He looked back along the aisle, and to his surprise the strange man had vanished. He looked around, certain that even Linford Christie himself wouldn't have been able to run out of sight so quickly, but there was no sign of the man at all.

"You were in a world of your own," Tommo chuckled as he set more boxes of Puffy Puff Puffs on the nearest shelf. "Thinking about that girl again?"

"Something like that," Josh replied, still watching the spot where the seemingly dead man had been standing. "Hey, do you ever seen anything unusual in here?"

"Always," Tommo said. "This one time, two kids came in with a lobster on a string, like they were walking it and -"

"I don't mean stuff like that," Josh said, interrupting him. "I mean stuff like..."

His voice trailed off as he realized that he

was about to open himself up to ridicule. After all, who would ever believe that a ghost might be haunting the brightest, brashest building in the entire town? Benson's Supermarket was a trashy and slightly rundown mecca to retail and commerce, and the idea of a ghostly spirit wandering along the aisles already felt increasingly daft. He looked again at the spot where the figure had been standing, and in that moment he told himself to put such foolish ideas out of his mind.

"Forget it," he murmured with a sigh, handing the cereal box back to his friend. "I've got to go, Gran gave me some jobs to do. Enjoy your Puffy Puff Puffs."

***

"And I told you," the man said, glaring up at Josh from his chair in front of the library's one public computer, "I'll be done when I'm done. I've got important business to take care of."

"Okay, fine," Josh replied, taking a step back, aware of a strangely fusty odor emanating from the fellow. "I'll... be around. Let me know when you're done."

Muttering something under his breath, the man returned his attention to the screen, which showed images of scantily-clad women that he appeared to be downloading and saving to a floppy drive. Josh looked around, surprised that anyone would do something like that in public, and then he wandered over to the nearest display of books. Figuring that he'd just have to wait until the guy was done getting photos, and wondering why the library didn't have a proper booking system for the computer or perhaps a time limit for individual sessions, he picked up some kind of old local history book by a guy named Ernest Dwyer and started flicking through the pages.

After a few minutes he glanced at the computer again, and he saw that the guy was now downloading blatant porn in broad daylight.

"Some people are crazy," he muttered, before looking at a poster by the door advertising a local exhibition of paintings by some guy named Anthony Toyner.

Looking back down at the book, he flicked to another page and found a section on local ghost stories. There was one about the pier, one about the old hotel near the castle, one about the castle itself and then – on the next page – one about the old school building. Those, Josh had to admit, seemed like *proper* locations for ghost stories, and there were certainly no tales about cafes, supermarkets or shoe shops. In fact, the more he leafed through Ernest Dwyer's book, the more Josh felt certain that the guy in the supermarket had probably been some old drunk who was fast on his feet, and the noises in the coffee shop late at night were probably caused by rodents.

"I'm telling you, you have to leave!" he heard a woman's saying firmly, and he turned to see that one of the librarians was in the process of throwing the strange guy off the computer. "You simply cannot do that sort of thing in public, Mr. Jefferson! If you don't leave right now, I shall have no choice but to call the police!"

CHAPTER FIVE

"I SAID – OH, NEVER mind!"

Realizing that the music was too loud to talk anyway, Josh turned and looked across Nelson's. The band on the stage was some local group that had recently formed following the demise of two other bands; the Crowford music scene was extremely close-knit and argumentative, and bands regularly changed members and even names as a result of small squabbles. Josh wasn't even a fan of this kind of hardcore punk sound, but at least local gigs gave him a chance to get out of the house, and most of the local pubs had stopped putting on nights.

"What do you think?" Lisa asked, nudging his arm.

Turning, he saw that she'd sidled over to

him yet again. Plenty of mutual friends had let him know that Lisa Winter had a crush on him, and he'd tried to tactfully let her know that he really wasn't interested. Now, as she grinned at him, he found himself wondering whether he should perhaps be a little more open-minded, but he realized after a few seconds that he was still too hung up on Sasha. Besides, Lisa was absolutely obsessed with cricket, and he knew that was one sport he could never pretend to like.

"All these bands kind of seem the same to me after a while," he replied, preferring to not commit to a firm opinion. "You know what it's like."

"Totally!" she said, staring at him with such intensity that he began to feel increasingly uncomfortable. "I don't like them either!"

Realizing that she was trying to get a conversation started, but having no idea what to say next, Josh looked around in the hope that he might spot someone who could help. Unfortunately everyone was watching the band on the stage, and after a few seconds Josh supposed that he needed to find some other way to get out of the awkward situation.

"Excuse me," he said, taking his beer from the bar and stepping past Lisa, "I just need to nip outside for a cigarette."

"I didn't know you smoked," she replied.

"It's never too late to give it a try," he said as he squeezed between two dancing girls and headed toward the door.

***

A cold wind blew along the seafront, rattling the flagpoles that stood at the entrance to the pier. Sheltering around the side of Nelson's, keen to stay slightly out of the way in case Lisa came looking for him, Josh listened to the sound of waves crashing against the beach in the dark of night.

Out at sea, a couple of red lights blinked in the distance, marking the positions of boats making their way along the English Channel.

"I could run away to sea," he mused, pondering his options. "That's what people did in the old days. Sometimes they were even kidnapped and press-ganged into work." He took a sip of beer. "That doesn't sound too bad right now. I could go on an adventure and come home twenty years later, full of new ideas."

He paused for a moment as the wind picked up, blowing some rain through the air.

"That's the problem with the modern day," he continued. "Everyone thinks it's so great that we get to choose what we want to do, but I'd actually quite like -"

Suddenly he heard a scream ringing out.

Turning, he looked along the alley that ran past the side of Nelson's, and he saw the artificially-lit car park a little further in the distance. He waited, telling himself that the scream had probably been nothing, but a moment later – above the muffled sound of music coming from inside the club – he heard footsteps hurrying across the car park, and sure enough a figure briefly ran past the end of the alley.

"Hey!" Josh called out, hurrying along the alley until he reached the car park, then looking out to see that only a handful of vehicles had been left overnight.

He looked over at the library, then at the back of one of the pubs, then at the far end of the car park, but he saw no sign of trouble. He knew from experience that while Crowford was a quiet town, people sometimes got into all sorts of scrapes late at night, especially; when alcohol was involved. Although the scream had been loud and piercing, he figured that it had probably just been the result of some local high jinks, and after a few seconds he took a sip of beer before turning to make his way back along the alley.

"Help me," a hushed, guttural voice groaned from somewhere nearby.

Startled, Josh looked back across the car park. He still couldn't see anyone, but now his mind was racing as he watched the shadows for any sign of movement.

"Hello?" he said cautiously, worried that someone might be hurt. "Is anyone there?"

He waited, but now he could hear a kind of harsh, rushed breathless sound, as if someone was struggling to get air into their lungs. He still couldn't actually see anyone, but he was more certain than ever that the voice had been real, and a moment later he spotted an old set of boxes that had been left piled up behind the rear gates of the *Admiral* pub. In that moment he realized that he could hear a shuffling sound coming from somewhere behind the boxes; as music continued to thud inside the club next door, he began to make his way past the boxes while preparing for the possible to turn and run.

"Hello?" he said again. "My name's Josh, I heard a noise and I just wanted to see whether everything's alright. If -"

Before he could finish, he saw a figure slumped on the ground, almost entirely hidden in the shadows.

"Help me," the figure whispered, and from his voice Josh could tell now that he was an old and perhaps very sick man. "Please, I've been here for so long."

As he felt the temperature in the air starting to drop, Josh swallowed hard; wind was blowing all around, howling along the various alleys that fed into the car park, and Josh couldn't help but notice that something about this man seemed unreal, as if he was trapped in shadows that were in some way part of his body.

"It's so dark," the man continued, his voice twisting in the cold dark air. "So very dark. I can't remember how long I've spent down here, but I don't know if I can ever get up again. What's it like, up there where you are in the light?"

"Up where I am?" Josh replied, struggling to shake a sense of unease. "I'm... not sure what you mean by that."

"I remember what it was like to be in the light," the man murmured, his voice starting to sound increasingly dark and gravely. "Now I'm down here and it's so very cold, and I can almost feel..." He paused for a moment, almost as if he was on the verge of fading away entirely. "I'm so cold," he added finally. "I don't think I'm supposed to be here."

"Can I help you?" Josh asked, still not quite ready to step forward and actually try to touch the man. "Is there someone I can call?"

"Call?"

"On a phone," he continued. "There's a payphone in the High Street, it's really close and I could -"

Suddenly the man began to get up, grabbing a railing on the wall in an attempt to steady himself.

Again Josh wanted to help, but he couldn't bring himself to get any closer to the man; even the thought of taking a step forward sent a shiver of fear through his chest, and he struggled to keep from turning and running away as the man hobbled out of the shadows.

"Now, then," the man murmured, as Josh saw his dark, angry eyes that seemed to be set a little too deeply into his sockets, "what's this all about, then? Where -"

In that moment, with no further morning, the man leaned forward and vomited, splattering the floor directly in front of Josh.

"Ken, are you out here?" a woman shouted, stumbling drunkenly around from the rear of Nelson's and then stopping as soon as she saw the man. "Oh, you're pissed!" she continued with a laugh, grabbing his hand and pulling him around the pile of vomit on the ground. "I wondered where you'd gone. Come on, let's get another drink inside you, that'll help."

"Evening, young chap," the man said, and now Josh saw that he was wearing a Ramones t-shirt as he was led by the hand back into the club. "Sorry about that. I fell over and it took me a while to get back up."

"It's fine," Josh said with a heavy sigh, "I just thought you were a ghost, that's all."

Left standing alone in the car park, Josh told

himself that this had been a useful lesson in credulity. He'd genuinely begun to worry that this 'Ken' fellow had been some kind of undead specter, but now he realized that he was merely another of Crowford's aging punks with a little too much of a liking for cheep beer. And as the stench of vomit began to reach his nostrils, and as he stepped back and began to make his way around to the club's front door, Josh tried to remember that the biggest danger in a town such as Crowford was his own overactive imagination.

CHAPTER SIX

"SO DIDN'T YOU SEE the last ever episode?" Lisa asked Josh a couple of hours later, as they and some friends headed out of Nelson's and began to make their way down into the High Street. "I know Alex Mack isn't the coolest show ever, but I always thought it was great."

"Huh," he replied, not even able to think of a better response.

"Is anywhere going to be open this late?" Harry called out from up ahead. "Come on, I'm not ready to go home yet! It's barely midnight!"

"We could go back to my place," Nabeel suggested. "Or we could go to the beach huts opposite the green."

"And freeze to death?" Tommo replied. "Seriously, between the lot of us can't we find one good place to hang out?"

"I recorded it," Lisa continued.

"Hmm?" Josh replied, having barely paid attention.

"The last episode of Alex Mack," she explained. "I recorded it, so if you wanted to come over one time and watch it, that'd be cool."

"I'm kind of busy," he said evasively as they walked past the shuttered Chinese takeaway and approached the traffic lights, which were still running through the cycle of colors despite the lack of cars. "Sorry."

"When?"

"When what?"

"When are you busy?"

"When you just said."

"I didn't say."

"Right," he continued, glancing at the window of the estate agent's office before spotting flashing blue lights further along the High Street. "That's..."

Stopping as most of the others carried on walking, Josh saw that an ambulance was parked further along the High Street, next to a police car. He told himself not to worry, but a moment later he saw a paramedic climbing out from the ambulance and carrying some kind of orange case into the shoe shop.

"What the hell?" he whispered.

"What's that?" Lisa asked, having made her way back to join him. "What's going on?"

"I don't know," he replied, hurrying along the High Street and breaking into a jog after a few paces.

"Wait for me!" Lisa called after him. "Josh? I can't run, remember? I'm really bad at running!"

Ignoring her completely, Josh hurried past the old phone box and stopped just in time to see two police officers emerging from the shoe shop. One of them was speaking into a radio, while the other stopped and looked back at the shop's front door.

"Is everything okay?" Josh asked, making his way over to the officer. "Did something happen?"

"Keep moving, Sir," the officer replied sternly. "We really don't need onlookers."

"I know people who work here," he explained, struggling to keep a sense of panic from his voice as he saw lots of lights inside the shoe shop. "Can you just tell me if anyone's hurt?"

Before the officer could say another word, Josh saw that a figure was being wheeled out of the shop on a stretcher. He craned his neck, trying to see past the paramedics and the various tubes attached to the figure, but after a moment he spotted Sasha's face. Without thinking, he pushed his way past the police officer and ran over to the stretcher, and to his immense relief he saw that while she was bloodied and bruised and clearly badly hurt, Sasha was at least alive and responsive.

"What happened?" he asked.

"Sir, you need to stay back," one of the paramedics said firmly.

"It got me," Sasha gasped, barely able to get any words out at all.

"Sir," the paramedic continued, putting a hand on Josh's arm, "I'm serious. She needs urgent medical attention."

"I saw it," Sasha said, as a police officer pulled Josh away. "It's real, Josh! I saw it and it's real, and it's angry! There's a ghost in there! Josh!"

Unable to follow, Josh watched helplessly as Sasha was loaded into the back of the ambulance. The lights of both the ambulance and a nearby police car were flashing out of sync, casting a constantly changing array of color an shadows across his face as Josh vaguely heard the police officer telling him insistently to get back behind the line of tape. Turning to look at the shoe shop again, he saw that the lights were now on, and that more police officers were picking their way past overturned sales stands that had been left scattered all across the floor.

"What the hell happened in there?" Josh whispered, feeling a growing sense of shock rippling through his chest. "What did this to her?"

***

"I'm sure your friend's gonna be fine," Tommo said an hour later, standing in his parents' kitchen with a can of beer in his hand. "Just call the hospital in the morning and check. They're not gonna tell you anything this late. Man, you don't even know which hospital she's been taken to. It might not be Crowford, she might have been taken to Dover or Canterbury."

"Something attacked her," Josh replied. "You didn't see the state of that place. It was like a bomb had gone off."

"What do you think it was?" Lisa asked, having stuck to Josh's side for most of the night. "Do you think it was, like, a wild dog or something?"

"She was trying to catch a ghost," Josh explained. "Well, not *catch* it exactly, but prove that it was real. I kind of made fun of her for it, I said ghosts wouldn't haunt a shoe shop. Looks like I was wrong."

"Maybe the ghost just got mad because she didn't have a pair of trainers in its size," Tommo suggested.

Josh turned and glared at him.

"But this isn't the time for humor," Tommo continued, clearly sensing that he'd got the tone wrong. He took a swig of beer from the can and mulled the situation over for a moment. "Man, this has been a crazy night. I can't believe an angry ghost might've gone on a rampage in the last shoe shop in Crowford. Hell, even the ghosts are struggling in this economy. If I was that ghost, I'd be feeling pretty sorry for myself, haunting a place where losers go to buy cheap shoes."

"It wasn't always a shoe shop," Josh pointed out. "It used to be part of Stryke Brothers."

"Which is?"

"It was this grand department store," Josh told him, "that took up a big chunk of the High Street back in the day. Apparently it was this dazzling place that sold almost anything you could want, but eventually the place failed and the building was sold off. Part of it was turned into the shoe shop, and part of it became Al's coffee shop. So whoever or whatever's haunting the shoe shop probably didn't start out when it was a shoe shop, they were probably haunting Stryke Brothers and then just sort of got... left behind when the place changed around them. It's a pretty crazy situation, if you really think about it."

"You'd think the ghost would get the message," Tommo suggested. "I mean, once the old department store had been gutted, wouldn't this ghost see that times are changing and the world's leaving them behind? What would even be the point of still haunting the place? Everywhere you looked, you'd see more and more reminders that the world you knew is gone. Hell, even the doors and windows wouldn't be in the right places. Wait, does this ghost walk straight through walls? That'd be so cool!"

"I don't know that they get much of a choice," Josh told him. "In fact, I'm sure they don't. But if there's a ghost there, it's been haunting the two shops for years without ever attacking someone. So why start now? What happened tonight that made it turn on Sasha?"

"Beats me," Tommo said with a shrug, before finishing his beer and crushing the can. "I'm sure someone'll go and clean it all up, though. This might've been the ghost's last hurrah. Now that it's finally had a go at a real living person, it'll probably just fade away to nothing. That's what ghosts do, right?" With that, he made his way through to the front room, where the others were playing a video game. "Hey, guys!" he called out. "Josh has just been telling me this totally nuts ghost story about the shoe shop in town! Do you wanna hear?"

"Something about this still doesn't quite add up," Josh said after a moment, still leaning against the kitchen counter. "Why would a ghost suddenly turn violent after years and years of being entirely passive?"

"I don't know," Lisa said cautiously, before

pausing for a few more seconds. "So do you want to come over tomorrow and watch the last episode of Alex Mack with me? I can get snacks!"

CHAPTER SEVEN

"ARE YOU WORKING AT the coffee shop today?" Evelyn asked, making her way back into the house from the garden with a bowl of freshly-cut tomatoes. "I can never remember your schedule. Why don't they just give you the same times each week?"

"Yeah, I'm on at three," Josh told his grandmother, as he looked through some CDs on the dining room table. "I have a few things to do before that, though. I'll be leaving just before lunchtime."

"Make sure you eat something."

"I will."

"I'll make you a sandwich," she continued, heading into the hallway. "You can take it with you and eat it when you get hungry. I hate to think of you running around out there and not slowing down to take care of yourself properly."

"Hey, Gran," Josh said, following her through to the kitchen, "you remember that Stryke Brothers department store, don't you?"

"Oh, it was wonderful," she replied with a smile as she opened the fridge door. "Your grandfather used to take me there sometimes for a treat. Not that we'd buy anything, of course. We couldn't afford most of the things they had, we were just from a mining family like so many of the families back then. But I remember one day when your grandfather bought a set of teaspoons from Stryke Brothers, I thought he was being so extravagant but he'd got a new job and he was earning more money, so he said we could afford to splash out now and again."

She set some things down on the counter, before opening the drawer and rooting through the cutlery. Finally she held up a somewhat stained old teaspoon.

"This is the only one of those six teaspoons that I've still got," she exclaimed proudly. "It might not look like much, but it's good quality and it's lasted me for decades."

"Were you sad to see Stryke Brothers shut down?"

"Oh, *very* sad," she said, "but it was a sign of the times. That, and the actual Stryke brothers didn't keep up with the times. Oswald Stryke was barely even there, he had other business interests. The shop was really the baby of Walter Stryke, everyone knew that he was in charge. Oswald kept him in check, but when he died, Walter was left to run the place all by himself. He had an eye for glamour and luxury, and I suppose he just went a little bit too far. People in Crowford liked buying nice things when they could afford them, but Walter's prices went up and up, and other shops opened nearby that sold the same things for far less." She paused for a moment. "Then there was poor Dorothy Maitland."

"Who was Dorothy Maitland?" Josh asked.

"I knew her, slightly," Evelyn told him. "She went for a job at Stryke Brothers, and then she vanished. Obviously no-one in their right mind believed that Walter had anything to do with it, but it was around that time that he seemed to lose his grip on the business. I think it was only about a year later that the signs went up, announcing one big final sale before Stryke Brothers shut its doors forever."

***

"No-one ever found Dorothy Maitland's body," Josh explained a couple of hours later, sitting in a chair next to Sasha's hospital bed. "Do you realize what that means? *She* might be the ghost that's haunting the shops today!"

"You make a good case," Sasha replied, clearly in pain as she lay back on the pillows, "but I don't see how it helps us. The thing that attacked me... it was definitely a woman, but I didn't get a good look at its face. It was at the top of the stairs and it just rushed at me, and I fell and... Well, look at me now. I'm lucky I didn't break even more bones!"

"How long had you spent trying to make contact with the ghost?"

"So long that I'd pretty much given up," she admitted. "I was just on my way back down from the stock room when I heard a noise over my shoulder. I turned to look, and that was when it rushed me."

"But you don't know it was truly attacking," he pointed out. "There might have been some kind of... misunderstanding."

"Are you giving the ghost the benefit of the doubt now?"

"Nan told me all about Dorothy Maitland's disappearance," he replied. "She went to Stryke Brothers to talk about a job, and that was the last anyone saw of her. Walter Stryke said she showed up and they talked, and he offered her the job, and then she left." He took Ernest Dwyer's book from his bag, having checked it out from the library.

Flicking through its pages, he found a photo showing the High Street back in the day, including a shot of Stryke Brothers. "Look," he continued, turning it around for Sasha to see, "that's what the place looked like."

"What's that behind it?" she asked.

Looking at the photo again, Josh saw the spire of a church rising up behind the store.

"That's some old church that used to be in the town," he told her. "It got bombed during the war, and then eventually the ruins were knocked down so they could build Benson's. A lot of people didn't like the idea of a church being cleared away to make space for a supermarket. Some of them, including Nan, still refuse to shop at Benson's as a matter of principle. They always go across the road instead."

"I admit that this Dorothy Maitland thing seems like a hell of a coincidence," Sasha told him, "but look at me, I'm in no position to go around hunting for ghosts. I think those days are behind me. I probably won't even get out of here in time to finish closing the shoe shop. I doubt anyone's going to bother now, so the place'll just stay shut until the end of the month, when a crew'll arrive to strip it down."

"Most likely no-one'll take the space over," he pointed out. "The shoe shop'll join the long line of empty spaces in the town. Soon the coffee shop'll be one of the last places that's open, and I'm not sure even Al's will last much longer."

"Look on the bright side," Sasha replied, "at least now you'll have time to sign up for college."

She started laughing, before letting out a gasp of pain.

"Broken rib!" she hissed. "Laughing makes it hurt like crazy!"

"Do you think Dorothy Maitland died at Stryke Brothers all those years ago?" Josh asked. "And if she did, is her ghost still haunting the place today?"

"I don't think I'm going to be able to find out," she said, before leaning over and opening the drawer in the table next to her bed. She searched around for something, clearly in pain, before taking out her wallet and leaning back against the pillow. "You're in luck, though," she continued through gritted teeth, as she slipped a key from the wallet and held it out for him to take. "If I'm right, that place is going to be empty now, all locked up and abandoned. That key's for the back door, and the number scratched onto the fob is all you need to turn the alarm off. So if you want to do some ghost-hunting, be my guest. Just don't forget to report back with your findings."

"I wouldn't even know where to start," he told her. "You're the expert in these things, and look how you wound up. Flat on your back in the hospital with a dozen broken bones."

"Which is why you have to be careful," she told him. "You also have to be smart. I think once I saw a ghostly figure walking through thin air near the shoe shop's top floor office. You need to try to track down and figure out the layout of the old department store, and see whether the ghost's still following any old routes. You also need to track down anyone who might still know what really happened to Dorothy Maitland. 1949 was slightly less than half a century ago, so it's not impossible that some of her friends are still alive. There might be some useful gossip that never made it into the official reports. Someone must have known something at the time. This is Crowford, after all. The entire town practically *runs* on gossip!"

"I don't know where I'd even start," he protested.

"Do I have to direct the operation from my hospital bed?" she asked with a sigh. "Dorothy Maitland would be in her eighties by now, right? So where in Crowford do people in their eighties tend to hang out the most? I'll give you a clue, it's not the pubs, and it's not Nelson's, and it's not any of the usual places we tend to go."

"Do you mean I have to trawl through the nursing homes?" he asked, showing no great enthusiasm for that prospect.

"That's one option," she told him with a

faint smile, "but first I'd go for the slightly easier option. Let me give you a hint. It's somewhere you've probably never been to before, and it's on Ward Street, right around the corner from where Stryke Brothers used to be. Hell, it's almost directly opposite Benson's, the supermarket. Oh, and dress light, because it's also one of the warmest places in the entire town."

CHAPTER EIGHT

"SIR," THE WOMAN BEHIND the desk said, looking up at Josh with a somewhat bemused expression, "this is Crowford Center for the Retired. You can't just walk in and start asking questions."

"All I need to do is see if anyone's memory might be jogged," he replied, adjusting his collar as he felt sweat starting to dribble down his back. "Can't I just... ask around and see if anyone knew Dorothy Maitland?"

"Our members come here to relax," she explained, "and to play card games, and to have something to eat and to be around like-minded individuals. They want to gently remember the good old days, not have their brains drilled for information about bad things that might have happened years ago. I'm sorry, but I can't just let you go charging into the place like that."

"It's really important," he told her.

"I'm sorry," she replied, "but you won't change my mind. Your questions could be very upsetting for our members, and if you don't leave immediately, I'll have to call the police. Have I made myself clear?"

Josh opened his mouth to reply to her, but at the last moment he merely sighed. Looking over at the doors that led into the retirement center's main area, he felt certain that somebody in there would be able to at least answer a few questions, but when he turned to the woman again he saw the fiery, determined expression on her face. Sure enough, a moment later she very deliberately reached over to the telephone on her desk.

"Well?" she continued. "Have I made myself clear, or do I need to get the police to explain my stance further?"

***

"I've tried every nursing home in town," Josh said a couple of hours later, as he examined a shirt in one of Crowford's many charity shops, "as well as the retirement center, and they all basically told me the same thing. I'm not even allowed to ask questions."

"That's too bad," Lisa said, holding up a dress. "What do you think of this? Should I try it on?"

"Do you know what's *really* weird?" Josh continued. "When I phoned them, most of the nursing homes rejected me with the exact same words. It was almost like they'd been told to expect my call, and they'd been given a script so they'd know what to say. Am I being totally paranoid, or do I have a right to feel like there's almost this..."

He paused, before turning to her as she held the dress against her body.

"Conspiracy?" he added cautiously.

"Hmm?" she replied, checking herself out in the mirror. "Does this make my hips look big?"

"Walter Stryke was apparently quite a powerful figure in the town for a while," Josh continued. "At one point he was even more powerful than the Grace family or the Archers, and those were always supposed to be the top dogs in Crowford over the years. But thanks to his department store, Walter Stryke was something of a celebrity. In fact, he paid actual celebrities to show up at the store and cut the ribbon every year when he launched his Christmas products. A guy like that must have had a lot of powerful friends."

"And enemies," Lisa pointed out. "I'm not sure about this dress. Does it look like something someone'd wear to a funeral?"

"Hear me out," Josh said. "What if Walter Stryke murdered Dorothy Maitland for some reason, and then he covered it up, and then the whole town – or at least the business community – closed ranks to cover it up? Walter Stryke has been dead for years, but it stands to reason that powerful interests might still not want to let the past get dredged up. What if, even after all these years, Walter Stryke is being protected?"

"It's quite expensive for second hand," Lisa said, holding the dress up again. "I don't know, I still kind of like it."

"You know who owns the retirement center, don't you?" Josh asked, heading over to the window and peering out. He could see the High Street and, beyond, the retirement center further along Ward Street. "The Grace sisters. Just like they own, or at least have owned in the past, half the town. I bet they own a bunch of the nursing homes as well, even though they pretend to be penny-pinchers. There's always been something weird about those two old women, they totally keep themselves to themselves. I bet they'd hate it to get out that they, or their family, had anything to do with protecting a murderer."

"I'm not going to get it," Lisa said, hanging the dress back on the rack but still staring at it. "Unless you think that I should. Do you think it'd look good on me, Josh? If I was wearing that dress, would you be embarrassed if we were... I don't know, on a date or something?"

"There are dark forces at work in this town," he murmured, still staring at the distant retirement center. "I can feel their tendrils oozing out everywhere. They want to keep their secrets hidden forever, and I'm not sure how far they'd go to achieve their goals. I might even be putting myself in great danger by asking too many questions and -"

Hearing the bell ring above the door, he turned to see that Lisa was storming outside.

"Where are you going?" he called out, hurrying after her, emerging into a light afternoon drizzle. "Hey, Lisa, what -"

"You're obsessed!" she snapped angrily, turning to him. "Do you realize that? You really can't think about anything else, can you? It's like you've watched too much *X-Files* and now you think there are conspiracies and secrets everywhere, but this obsession isn't healthy. It's going to drive you mad!"

"Sasha thinks the ghost in the shoe shop is connected to the disappearance of Dorothy Maitland forty-nine years ago," he told her.

"And that's what this is about, isn't it?" she replied, with the first hint of tears in her eyes. "Are you trying to discover the truth about Dorothy Maitland's death, or are you just trying to impress Sasha? Because from where I'm standing, it seems to me that you've got a massive crush on her, and you're completely blind to the fact that she's not interested in you!"

"That's a little harsh," he murmured.

"You haven't stopped talking about her once today," she told him. "Meanwhile, you haven't even asked me how I am!"

"Well, I didn't think I need to," he stammered.

"It's my birthday!" she hissed.

"Oh."

"Forget it," she replied, turning and walking away down one of the alleys that led to the car park. "I should have known better than to think that you'd even remember!"

Josh could still hear her ranting to herself as she hurried off into the distance. He briefly considered running after her and apologizing, but at the last minute he realized that there was really no point. He'd always felt that girls could be very difficult to understand, and Lisa was perhaps the most girly girl he'd ever met; he told himself that he had no hope of ever understanding what was going on in her mind, but also that she'd eventually calm down and start acting normally again, and that she might even be big enough to apologize.

"See you around, then," he murmured, even though she was long gone.

Checking his watch, he saw that he still had forty-five minutes until he was due to start his shift at the coffee shop. Sometimes he went in early and had a drink before changing into his uniform, but on this occasion he was starting to realize that there might be a much better use for his time. With light rain still falling but not really threatening to become anything more serious, he looked along the High Street and thought of two particular houses that might be interesting. After checking his watch again, just to be sure that he had enough time, he began to make his way toward the north end of town.

Passing the *Red Cow* pub, he saw posters for various bands put together by his friends. He made his way past the memorial to the victims of the Mercy Belle disaster, and a few minutes later he passed the grand old house that he knew – from his research into the town's history – had once belong to the famous (or infamous) Milligan family. Finally, reaching the end of Baker Street, he stopped and glanced over his shoulder. He knew that he was almost certainly not being followed, yet he couldn't entirely erase a glimmer of fear from his mind. Deep down, he felt certain that he was on the verge of interfering in a deep and very secret part of Crowford's history.

Heading along Baker Street, he saw the shuttered and abandoned *Crowford Hoy* pub ahead, but he took the next right turn and made his way instead along Nelson Street. Finally, slowing his pace, he saw the two houses ahead, facing one another. He stopped a little way short of the houses, and he couldn't help but feel a flicker of fear in his belly as he saw the red door of number fourteen and the black door of number fifteen. Behind those doors, he knew, lived Angela and Vivian Grace.

CHAPTER NINE

AS SOON AS HE'D knocked on the black door of number fifteen, Josh realized that he was making a terrible mistake. His confidence fell away and he felt an urge to run, but a moment later he heard a shuffling sound from the other side of the door and he realized that running would only make things seem worse.

Finally the door inched open, and a woman's face appeared. As soon as he saw her, Josh knew that this was the mysterious and supposedly reclusive Vivian Grace.

"Hello," he said, unable to hide the fear in his voice, "you don't know me, but I'm... doing some research into local history and I was wondering whether I could talk to you about something."

He waited, but she merely continued to stare at him.

"I tried your sister's door first," he explained, nodding back toward the red-doored house opposite, "but she, uh... I suppose she wasn't in."

Again he waited, and he was already fairly certain that he was going to get absolutely nowhere. Vivian Grace was well into her seventies, and Josh had heard the rumors about her having spent time at various hospitals over the years; in fact, as he tried to think of some way to extract himself from the awkward situation, he began to hope that she really didn't even know what was happening.

"I was just hoping to ask you about someone named Dorothy Maitland," he added finally, supposing that he might as well watch to see if she reacted. "She lived here a long time ago, back in the 1940s. I think... she might have been about the same age as you?"

Keeping his eyes fixed on Vivian's face, he saw not even the slightest flicker of recognition. A moment later, however, he heard a woman's muffled voice saying something inside the house. Vivian half-turned to look back inside, and then – without saying anything else – she gently bumped the door shut, leaving a rather relieved Josh standing in the drizzle on the Nelson Street pavement.

"Okay, I'm sorry to have disturbed you," he

said after a few more seconds, before turning and walking away, convinced that he'd just had a very near miss. "Let's just... pretend that this never happened."

***

"Are you just going to stand there all day?" Betty asked, tapping Josh on the shoulder. "Or are you perhaps actually thinking of doing some work around here?"

Startled, he turned to her and saw that she'd made her way along the counter. Having been in the process of cleaning out the filters on the two coffee machines, Josh had instead become somewhat focused on something else entirely; looking back up, he once again saw the faintest ridges running across part of the ceiling.

"What are you doing?" Betty sighed. "We need those filters cleaned, ready for the four o'clock rush."

"I know," he replied, before pointing at the ceiling, "but do you know what those are?"

"Should I?"

"I think they're left over from when this place used to be Stryke Brothers," he explained. "I've been trying to make sense of the layout back then, it's not easy but I *think* the main staircase used to run up the center, which means half of it would have been in here and half would have been in the shoe shop next door."

"And how does that help us?" she asked.

He turned to her again.

"You need to get your head out of the clouds," she said firmly, prodding his chest with one bony finger. "No-one cares what Al's used to be back in the day. To be perfectly honest with you, I'm far more concerned with the questions of what it's going to be a year from now. In case you hadn't noticed, shops in this town are dropping like flies, and if no-one's coming down the High Street to buy things, then no-one's going to need coffee, are they?"

"You raise a good point."

"I know," she said, turning and shuffling back over to the till. "I always do, it's just that other people so rarely bother to listen. If people actually listened to me, we'd get so much more work done and we'd be so much more efficient, but it's almost as if my voice just goes in one ear and out the other with most people. I'm used to it, of course, but that doesn't make it any less frustrating. Sometimes I think there might be something actively wrong with my voice, like something about the frequency that makes it easier for people to ignore what I'm saying."

She was still talking at length, about something or other, as Josh returned his attention to the ceiling. The more he looked around the coffee shop, the more he realized that he could see little hints of the old layout slowly emerging from behind the plaster and paint. The signs were subtle, which he reasoned explained why he'd never noticed them before, but he had no doubt that the conversion job had been done incredibly cheaply; looking toward the storeroom, he saw the strange wall that ran almost diagonally across the space, and which had never really made much sense to him, and he understood now that this must have been some dodgy builder's way of quite literally cutting corners. The more he looked at the layout of the cafe, the more he saw the bones of the original building starting to show through.

"But that's the thing about salt," Betty was saying as Josh finally noticed her voice again, "you don't need all this fancy stuff when bog standard salt'll do the job. Don't you think?"

"Absolutely," he replied, not really knowing what she was on about. "Sorry, do you mind if I go and grab something from the back?"

Even as she replied, he was already making his way through into the storeroom. Although he wasn't entirely sure what he was looking for, he felt as if he was seeing hints of the past emerging through the lurid patterns of the coffee shop's walls. The farthest wall, in fact, was covered in large orange spirals that extended all the way through the shop to the front windows. Josh had seen those spirals thousands of times, he knew the pattern better than he knew the back of his own hand, yet now he found himself staring at them almost as if he was hypnotized. No matter how hard he tried to look away, he felt as if he was being drawn into the design at the same time as his thoughts began to melt away.

Meanwhile, the wall to his left began to bulge slightly, as if the original layout of the building was attempting to reassert itself.

"Josh?"

Startled by a hand touching his elbow, Josh spun around and stepped back. In the process, he knocked a metal tray off the side, sending several cups crashing and smashing down against the floor.

"What's going on with you today?" Betty asked. "What were you doing in here?"

"I was just... fetching something," he told her.

"Fetching something? For half an hour?"

"What?"

Glancing at his watch, he saw that the time was almost five past four. Looking toward the door, he realized that he could hear lots of voices in the coffee shop, including the usual screaming children. He knew that something had to be wrong, that the time had only been quarter to four when he'd made his way into the storeroom, but in that case he had no idea how almost twenty minutes could have passed in the blink of an eye.

"I haven't had a chance to sit down," Betty complained. "I called through to you and you kept saying you were coming. What were you really doing?"

"I spoke to you?" he replied, shocked by that suggestion.

"Give me strength," she said, rolling her eyes as she headed back through to the counter. "Get a move on, or I'll have to put in a report saying that you're slacking on the job. I don't want to do something like that, Josh, but if you keep acting like this you'll leave me no choice."

Taking a deep breath, Josh tried to pull his thoughts together, but he still felt strangely bemused. He looked at the pattern on the wall again, and he tried to work out just how he could possibly have mesmerized by something so ridiculous. Stepping over to the wall, he reached out and touched the pattern, and he couldn't shake the feeling that – at least for a few minutes – his mind somehow hadn't been his own.

"Josh?" Betty yelled from behind the counter. "Are you doing it again?"

"No!" he blurted out, turning and hurrying out to join her. "Sorry, no, of course not. I'm right here. What do you need me to do first?"

AMY CROSS

CHAPTER TEN

"THANKS, MRS. WINTER," JOSH said as he sat at the bottom of the stairs, with the phone's receiver against his ear, "but could you just give my message to Lisa, please? And tell her..."

His voice trailed off for a moment as he thought back to the sight of Lisa storming out of the charity shop earlier.

"Tell her I'm sorry if I was rude today," he added. "She'll know what I mean by that."

Once the call was over, he set the receiver down and leaned back against the stairs. He knew he'd been mean to Lisa and somewhat dismissive; while he sometimes found her a little dull, he knew she was as good friend and he desperately wanted to make things up to her. As he stared at the wall, however, he found himself thinking back to the coffee shop, and to the patterns on the walls, and he once again felt his mind starting to empty, to the extent that he barely even heard the doorbell ring or noticed his grandmother shuffling through to greet their visitor. He was still lost in his own world a couple of minutes later when, finally, he felt a hand nudging his shoulder.

"Josh, are you completely out of it today?" Evelyn asked, clearly concerned by her grandson's mood. "Josh, I've been calling through to you. Someone's here to see you and, well..."

She turned and looked toward the door that led into the living room, and for a moment she seemed extremely troubled.

"What have you been up to?" she continued finally, turning to him. "Why is *she* here?"

***

"My Josh is a good boy," Evelyn said a few minutes later, as she sat in the front room, "and I really don't know what any of this is about. He'd never get into any trouble."

"Nevertheless," Angela Grace said, keeping her eyes fixed on Josh, "he turned up unannounced at my sister's house today and caused her a great deal of distress."

"I didn't mean to upset anyone," Josh explained, still somewhat shocked to find himself talking to this infamous and supposedly rather reclusive member of one of Crowford's most famous families. "I just knocked on her door to see if she could help me with some research. I knocked on your door first, M'am, but you weren't home so..."

His voice trailed off.

"Vivian is not supposed to receive callers," Angela said firmly. "My sister has led a very troubled life, and although we don't see one another very often, we..." She paused for a moment, before sighing and shaking her head. "I hardly need to go into these personal matters," she added. "Suffice it to say that no-one should ever go knocking on her door like that. I thought everyone in Crowford was aware of our need for privacy."

"Yes, Josh," Evelyn said firmly, "everyone in Crowford should know by now that that Grace family prefers not to be bothered. I really don't understand what you could have been thinking."

"Vivian has been subjected to so much scurrilous gossip over the years," Angela continued, "and I simply won't allow such things. I want to make it very clear, young man, that any further attempts to contact my sister or my family will result in police involvement."

"Everyone's very keen to call the police all of a sudden," Josh murmured.

"What was that?" Angela asked.

"Nothing," he replied.

"I hope I've made my point," Angela said, getting to her feet.

"Oh, absolutely," Evelyn said, standing and hurrying past so that she could open the door for her. "I'm so dreadfully sorry that you felt the need to come here this evening, I hope it wasn't too much of an inconvenience."

"An inconvenience?" Angela replied archly. "Why, of course it was an inconvenience. How could it not have been?"

Josh opened his mouth to apologize yet again, but at the last second he held back. His grandmother had been almost groveling ever since Angela Grace had set foot in the house; indeed, he could hear Evelyn still saying sorry over and over again, begging for forgiveness in a manner that Josh was frankly starting to find rather overbearing. Sure, the Grace family had once been very well-known in Crowford, but their grander days were behind them and as he stood up and headed to the hallway Josh felt as if they didn't quite deserve so much reverence. In fact, in that moment he was quite keen to puncture Angela Grace's balloon of pomposity and self-importance.

"Dorothy Maitland," he said as he saw Angela stepping outside.

Turning, Angela stared back at him.

"It was about Dorothy Maitland," he

continued, aware that he'd gone too far to back down now. "She used to work at -"

"I know who she was," Angela replied, cutting him off. "Ms. Maitland's disappearance was quite the story back in... I believe it was the late 1940s."

"1949, to be precise," Josh told her. "She vanished after going to a job interview at Stryke Brothers."

"My family has been involved in many aspects of Crowford life," Angela said with a forced smile, "but Stryke Brothers was entirely a venture run by Walter and Oswald Stryke. Their rather tawdry department store had absolutely nothing to do with the Graces."

"But you're well-connected, right?" Josh continued. "Or at least, you used to be, back in the day."

"I'm not sure that I like either your implication or your tone," Angela said firmly.

"He's not trying to cause trouble," Evelyn replied, clearly trying to reassure their visitor. "Josh, perhaps -"

"I just wondered," Josh continued, interrupting his grandmother as he watched Angela's face closely for any sign of a clue in her expression, "whether you or your sister ever heard anything about Dorothy Maitland, or about what happened to her. If there was any gossip back then,

I'm sure the most important people in town would have been all over it."

"There was no gossip," Angela said curtly. "At least, not as far as I control. Besides, Dorothy Maitland's disappearance occurred many years ago, and I'm sure the police looked into it at the time. Why would anyone be wanting to dig up all that old business now?"

"I'm interested in the history of this town," he told her.

"That's a very commendable hobby," she replied, "but I would caution against trying to turn your hobby into anything more. There are some very interesting and well-written books in the library about Crowford's history. If I were you, I'd stick to reading those."

"Do you mean the ones sponsored by your family?" he asked, with the bit between his teeth now. "Are you sure they haven't been carefully sanitized? After all, I'd have thought that one of the key elements of any historical investigation is hearing different viewpoints."

"My," Angela replied, "you're really a very intelligent young man, are you not? It's been a while since anyone went snooping around like this, you could probably do very well as a journalist. If Mr. Faraday was still with us, I would most certainly pass your details to him. As it stands, however, you'll probably have most success plying your trade in London or beyond. There's certainly nothing worth investigating here in Crowford. This is just a sleepy little English seaside town."

"I'll be the judge of that," Josh told her.

"I think what my grandson means," Evelyn said cautiously after a moment, "is that he's grateful for your compliment, and he'll refrain from bothering anyone again. He's certainly a very good boy."

"Yes, you keep saying that," Angela replied. "I do hope that you're correct."

With that she turned and made her way outside, leaving Evelyn to shut the door and let out a big sigh of relief.

"What were you thinking?" she asked finally, turning to her grandson. "Do you know who that is? It's Angela Grace, one of the richest women in all of Crowford!"

"She didn't look very rich to me," he replied. "And if she's got so much money, what are she and her sisters doing living in little houses on opposite sides of Nelson Street? Has she got all her money hidden under her mattress or something like that?"

"I don't want you to cause any more trouble, Joshua," she said firmly, raising a finger and jabbing it toward his face. "Do you hear me? I can't believe Angela Grace herself had to come to our house to sort this out." She made her way past him, heading back into the front room. "I forgot to put *Emmerdale* on to record, but I should be able to catch the last few minutes. My heart's racing at a million miles an hour, Joshua, you really mustn't do this sort of thing to me. I don't want any more surprises. Is that understood?"

"Absolutely," he replied, even though deep down he was already making other plans. "Don't worry, Gran. I'll make sure I don't attract any more attention."

CHAPTER ELEVEN

"HELLO," JOSH SAID THE following night, standing in the shoe shop well after dark, having let himself in with Sasha's key. "Are you here? Can you hear me? If there's a ghost here, you need to come out. I want to talk to you."

He waited, but in truth he hadn't really expected this approach to work. He'd only been inside the shop for a few minutes, and so far the place seemed empty and deserted, although he couldn't quite shake a sense that he was being watched. Really, his opening speech had mainly been an attempt to set the scene, to let the ghost know that he meant business, and now he was going to get on with the main part of his plan, which meant -

Hearing a knocking sound, he turned to see

a figure banging gently on the door. He made his way over and turned the key, and after pulling the door open he found himself face-to-face with Lisa Winter.

"You came," he said, a little surprised to see her.

"My mum gave me your message," she told him. "Why did you want to meet me here?"

"Meet you?" He paused. "I called to apologize."

"Yeah, and then you said you wanted me to come down here tonight to meet you." She pushed past him, stepping into the shop and rubbing her hands together. "It's so cold out there. Don't you have any heating on?"

"Whatever," her replied, closing and locking the door again. "And no, there's no heating. This place is pretty much being run into the ground before it closes for good."

"Are we allowed to be here?" she asked, looking at the racks of shoes in the darkness. "Did you get permission?"

"I... didn't break in," he told her.

"This is so cool," she continued, turning to him with a grin. "We're like detectives!"

"I'm not sure we're exactly like detectives," he replied, making his way past her, picking his way over some old stands that had been left all over the floor. "Ghost-hunting can be a lonely business, and

I suppose I just wanted to have someone here to verify what I think I see or hear." He stopped and looked over at the checkout for a moment. "I think so, anyway," he added under his breath, before turning to her. "Are you *sure* I told your mum that you should come here tonight?" he added. "I really don't remember that."

"Do you want me to leave?"

"No, not really. Sorry, I suppose my head's in a weird place right now. You wouldn't believe some of the stuff that's been happening over the last few days."

"Try me."

"It'd take too long to explain," he told her, "and you probably wouldn't understand anyway."

"Okay," she said meekly, looking down at her own feet. "I'm sorry, I just thought when you asked me to come, it might be because you wanted to... hang out."

"That ghost attacked Sasha," he replied, "which means it *can* be provoked. It's aware of modern people in the present day, even if it ignores them most of the time. We have to try to use that fact to our advantage."

"How?"

"I think the ghost is trapped," he continued. "It's looping somehow, it's doing the same things over and over again, so we have to break that loop so that it notices us. We have to piss it off."

"Are you sure that's a good idea?" she asked.

"Not particularly," he said, unable to hide the fear in his voice, "but at least there are two of us here tonight, so we have a better chance. Fortunately, I think I know exactly where to begin."

***

"So," Lisa said a couple of hours later, as they sat together on two chairs behind the desk in the shoe shop's office upstairs, "when you said earlier that you had a plan... was it just to sit around doing nothing?"

"We need to get a glimpse of the ghost first," he told her.

"Why?"

"It's like unraveling a carpet," he continued. "First you need to find a loose thread. Think of the ghost as a loose thread in a much larger mystery."

"Okay," she said, furrowing her brow for a moment. "I get it. I think. But what exactly are we waiting for? A moaning sound? A loose floorboard creaking in the dead of night?"

"You're thinking about cliched horror movies," he told her. "Does this seem like a cliched horror movie? When you look around, do you see cobwebs and candles and creepy old rooms?"

"No."

"What do you see?"

"Cheap shoes, remainder bins and adverts."

"Precisely," he continued, "so we need to think outside the box." He paused for a moment, watching the side of her face. "You know," he added, "this is actually a really big opportunity. We could be on the verge of making a massive discovery, and I'm letting you join me at ground zero of the entire thing. Do you have any idea how famous we'll both be if we manage to get even the tiniest sliver of proof?"

"I'm not sure that I want to be famous," she told him. "It seems stressful."

"You should show a little more gratitude," he replied, still watching her carefully. "I didn't have to invite you along tonight."

"I thought you barely remember that you *did* invite me."

"That's not the point," he said firmly, "and you know it. How can you not be in awe of what we're about to do here? We're dealing with something that spans the worlds of the living and the dead, with something that's echoing through to us across five decades. Sure, this just looks like some old shoe shop, but when you really study the walls you'll start to see little hints of what used to be here. This was once a wonderful old department store, it was a jewel in the crown not only of Crowford but of the entire Kent coast. People would flock to Stryke Brothers to see the latest fashions, to buy the newest gadgets and... hell, they'd even come here just to be seen, just so they could tell their friends they stepped foot in the place. Even daring to walk through the door showed that you were a certain type of person!"

"It did?" she replied skeptically.

"If you could see this place in its heyday," he continued, getting to his feet and stepping out across the office before turning to her, "you'd be blown away. I know it's easy to be cynical in this day and age, but is it so hard to believe that at one time Crowford was actually ahead of its time?"

"I'm not sure," she said awkwardly, glancing around again. "I'm still really cold. We're not going to stay here all night, are we? What time are we going to call it quits? Midnight?"

She checked her watch.

"It's only ten now," she added, before breathing extra hard into the air. "I can see my breath!"

"You need to open your mind to this experience," he told her.

"Well, if there's a ghost here," she replied, "then where is it? Is it shy?"

"We stand on the verge of greatness," he told her, "and you want instant gratification. That's kind of sad, if you ask me, but it's also a sign of the times. Fortunately you've come to the right place tonight, because I'm going to educate you so that you're just a little more grateful."

"Josh -"

"Don't interrupt me," he added, stepping closer to her and staring down as she remained in her chair. "You're a pretty girl, Lisa," he said, "but you're also a little plain, and sometimes you come across as being... I don't want to say stupid, I truly don't, but you're not giving me a lot to work with here. You can be cloth-eared at times, but as my brother always says, there's no-one in this world who can't be changed if you just give them a push. Of course, he's talking about me most of the time, but there's still some logic to his argument."

"I didn't know you had a brother," she said, clearly a little bemused. "And why are you calling me plain? I don't think that's fair, Josh. Besides, you're not exactly the most fashionable guy in the world!"

"The whole world is your oyster, Dorothy," he continued, fixing her with a determined stare that made her feel distinctly uncomfortable. A moment later he reached over and took hold of her hand, squeezing it gently before placing his other hand on her waist. "I'm giving you something wonderful," he added with a smile. "Something that no other man in all of Crowford can give you, Dorothy. I mean... Lisa. The question now becomes... what are you going to give me in return?"

AMY CROSS

CHAPTER TWELVE

"WHAT DID YOU JUST say to me?" Lisa asked, staring at Josh with a growing sense of disbelief. "Did you..."

As her voice trailed off, she tried to work out whether he was serious.

"You heard me," he replied, still staring down at her. "This is the opportunity of a lifetime, and I think you should show a little gratitude. You were brought up properly, weren't you? Please, tell me that your parents raised you to show respect."

"They did, as it happens," she said, standing just inches from him now. "They also raised me to tell people like you where to go."

"People like me?"

"I didn't think you were like this, Josh," she continued, struggling to hold back tears. "Damn it, why am I always such a bad judge of character? Out of all the guys I ever hang out with at Nelson's, why did I have to convince myself that you were the most decent?"

"I fear you're getting confused," he replied, reaching out and taking hold of her wrist. "My dear, let us try to -"

"Don't touch me!" she snapped, slapping him hard and then pulling free, hurrying toward the stairs. "I don't want anything to do with you!"

"You'll regret that," Josh muttered, turning and rushing after her, chasing her down the stairs and into the darkened sales floor of the shoe shop. "Get back here and apologize to me immediately!"

"Never!" she gasped, running through to the back of the shop and past the storeroom, then opening the back door and hurrying out into the yard at the edge of the car park. "If you touch me, I'll scream!"

"I'll do more than touch you!" Josh shouted after her. "When I get my hands on you, I'll make you wish you'd never come here tonight! I'll make you wish you'd never even heard of Stryke Brothers!"

Stumbling and almost tripping over some boxes, Josh nevertheless managed to keep pace with Lisa as she ran out across the car park. With no cars having been left overnight, the wide empty space was bathed in an orange glow. Although there were three exits, Lisa chose instead to run directly toward the rear of Benson's, slamming against the staff door and trying to pull it open, only to find that it was locked.

"Help me!" she sobbed as she heard Josh racing up behind her. "Somebody please -"

As soon as Josh grabbed her arm from behind, she turned and screamed, swinging a punch and whacking his jaw. He crumpled immediately, letting out a pained gasp as she stepped closer and kicked him in the belly.

"Lisa, stop!" he shouted, clearly in agony as he held a hand up to stop her. "Lisa, it's me!"

"You can keep your job!" she shouted, kicking him again, this time in the shoulder. "I wouldn't work for you, Mr. Stryke, for all the money in the world!"

"Lisa, listen to my voice!" Josh hissed, flinching as he pulled back from her. "Lisa, something's really wrong here! We're not being ourselves!"

***

"I think it started this afternoon," he said a few minutes later, still winded and in pain, as they sat on the grass outside the rear of the supermarket, staring out at the car park. "For me, at least. I was in the coffee shop and I felt like I was almost...

hypnotized."

"I was Dorothy Maitland," Lisa replied, furrowing her brow. "Wasn't I? It's like someone else's thoughts were in my head, it's almost as if I was..."

She struggled to complete that sentence, even though she knew the word she should use. When she turned to Josh, she saw in his eyes that he was thinking the same thing.

"Possessed," they both said at the same time.

"I would never act like that," Josh added, getting to his feet and taking a step back. "Lisa, you have to believe me, I'm not some kind of creep."

"I know," she replied.

"I'm just not like that," he continued, clearly on the verge of panic. "I would never, in a million years, lure anyone to some confined space and then try to make advances on them. I don't have that in me, I'd rather... I'd rather die!"

"And I'd never kick and punch someone unless I really thought my life was in danger," she told him. "Which I don't think I did. I mean, I *did*, but it's like that sense came from somewhere outside my body."

"We were reenacting what happened that night," Josh replied.

"What do you mean?"

"I know this is going to sound crazy," he

continued, holding his hands up, "but I think I was possessed by the ghost of Walter Stryke, and you were possessed by the ghost of Dorothy Maitland, and we were somehow... replaying the events that led to her disappearance. Or, as looks increasingly likely, her death." He looked around for a moment, before pointing to one of the exits. "Look," he added, "there are three ways out of this car park. One leads onto Ward Street, one leads past Benson's and out onto the road near the train station and one goes past the back of the old furniture shop and onto St. Dunstan's. In fact, there's even a fourth if you go around the side, you could go past the back of that old sweet shop."

"What are you trying to say?"

"I'm saying that you have so many ways to escape from me, but you didn't choose any of them," he pointed out, before turning to look at the metal door at the rear of the supermarket. "Why were you trying to get in there?"

"I don't know," she admitted.

"Isn't it obvious? That must be where Dorothy ran on the night Walter attacked her."

"Into the supermarket."

"Only it wasn't a supermarket back then," he pointed out. "It was a church, wasn't it? There was a church here, it got bombed in the war and then it stood empty for a while in ruins, and then it got knocked down and the supermarket was built here.

That's why my grandmother refuses to shop here, she thinks it was wrong to get rid of the church." She stared at the door for a moment longer. "But back in 1949, when Dorothy Maitland ran for her life from the back of Stryke Brothers, there might well have been all sorts of walls where those exits are now. So she ran into the ruins of the church."

"That... kind of makes sense," Lisa admitted. "In a weird sort of way, at least. But what does it mean? Wouldn't they have searched inside the church when she went missing?"

"Of course," he replied, "but maybe not that thoroughly, not if they didn't really think she'd gone in there."

"So... was her ghost trying to show us something tonight?" Lisa asked.

"It's almost as if they're both trying to show us something," he told her, "but I don't quite understand the part with Walter Stryke. I looked into him, he eventually moved away from Crowford after the department store closed down and he died just a few years ago in Canada. I even managed to track down a picture of his gravestone out there, so how could *his* ghost be haunting a building in Crowford?"

"Is there some rule about where ghosts are allowed to haunt?"

"There's something we're missing," he continued, "and whatever it is, I think tonight

Dorothy Maitland was trying to show us."

"I can't believe we were possessed," she said, as a shiver ran through her body. "Wait, how do we know we're not possessed right now? What if those ghosts take control of us again?"

"I felt wrong all day," he told her, "but now I'm feeling quite a bit better. I know it's weird, but I think I can sort of tell the difference."

"Yeah," she replied after a moment's consideration, "I think I can too. At least, I hope so."

"I'm really truly sorry for how I behaved," Josh said, before shaking his head. "I don't know if I can ever make it up to you, but I hope you realize that I never in a million years would have done any of that if Walter hadn't been controlling me. Honestly, there's nothing that could ever make me try to make a move on you like that. I'd rather die."

"Thanks," she said, forcing a smile. "I think."

"The shoe shop shuts at the end of the month," he continued, turning to at the supermarket's staff door again, "and after that happens, I probably won't be able to get inside again. That means there's a limit to what we can do here, and a limit to how long we've get left. If we don't figure out what happened to Dorothy Maitland by the end of the month, and where and how she died, the mystery might remain a mystery forever."

He paused, still staring at the door. "Somebody has to know something. People can try to keep secrets in this town all they want, but the truth has to come out somehow. There has to be someone who knows what really happened."

CHAPTER THIRTEEN

"ELIZABETH BARRINGTON STRYKE," SASHA said, sitting up in her hospital bed the following day. "Or Elizabeth Barrington Todlover, as she was born. Todlover, huh? You can see why she'd want to change that name in a hurry."

"Walter Stryke's wife?" Josh said, looking at the photocopied page from some old book. "How does this help us?"

"Her marriage to Walter Stryke fell apart in the 1950s, not long after Dorothy Maitland disappeared," Sasha explained. "She cited estrangement and abandonment in her divorce petition. That was actually a pretty tough time for the Stryke family as a whole, because Walter's brother Oswald died. The business empire fell apart, and Walter ended up going to live in Canada. But if anyone would know what really happened, it's his ex-wife, and the bonus is that she seems to have severed all ties with Crowford after the divorce, so it's not like she'd be easily shut up by the Graces."

"She'd be a hundred years old by now," Josh pointed out.

"Sure, if old Walter didn't like his ladies slightly on the young side." She handed him another photocopy. "My mother was busy on the library photocopier yesterday. It seems that Elizabeth was barely of legal age when she married Walter, so actually she's still alive. And there's another bonus, because -"

"Does she still live in Crowford?" he asked eagerly. "That's amazing! That's the break we've been looking for!"

"Not quite," she replied. "She's not far away, though. So tell me, how would you fancy a day-trip to London? Not with me, of course. My legs are still broken, and I honestly don't think I'm going to be up and about for at least a month or two. So do you think you can make it up to Marble Arch by yourself?"

***

"Thanks for coming," Josh said several hours later, as he and Lisa stood in the packed underground carriage, pulling out from Charing Cross. "You didn't have to, you know."

"And miss a trip to the big city?" she replied. "You're not the only one who got possessed last night. I'd kind of like to know more about who slipped me on like a glove, and why. Plus, I've been meaning to take a trip to a couple of my favorite comic shops. My birthday money's been burning a hole in my pocket for months."

"You like comic shops?" he replied with a raised eyebrow.

"What's *not* to like?" she asked as the train rumbled into the tunnel and the lights briefly flickered. "Okay, fine, you think I'm really sad and I get that, but some of us like to have actual, cool hobbies. Don't worry, though, I'm used to getting looked down on. Your friend Sasha called me a geek once."

"She probably wasn't trying to be mean," he told her. "Or you misheard."

"You really like her, don't you?" she continued, with a hint of disappointment in her voice. "It's okay, I've noticed the way you talk about her. Why don't you tell her?"

"She'd never like me," he replied.

"Why not?"

"Because she's too cool," he explained. "And smart. And funny. And hot. It's okay, I came to accept the truth a while ago. The only girls who'd ever like me are dorky, boring people with bad dress sense and no other options."

"Huh," she replied, looking the other way along the carriage for a moment in an attempt to hide her expression. "I suppose you might be right." She sniffed back the first possibility of tears for a moment, before turning to him again with a big, broad smile. "Do you know what I think?" she asked. "I think words like geek and nerd are used as insults right now, but one day they'll be compliments."

"How do you reckon that's going to happen?"

"I don't know," she said with a shrug, "but I just think the world's going to change. Comics are cool, and eventually the world's going to catch up to that fact. Take some of the biggest comic book heroes around. Sure, most comic book movies these days look kind of lame, but one day the special effects are going to be incredible and then people won't laugh at those stories. One day, comic book movies are going to be huge mainstream hits."

"Now you're just dreaming," he suggested with a smile. "I'm not criticizing you, by the way, but I think you need to be realistic and keep your feet on the ground."

"You'll see that I'm right eventually," she said with a faint, knowing smile as she looked up at the tube map on the carriage wall. "So we have to change to get to Marble Arch, right? Tottenham

Court Road for the Central Line?"

***

"These houses are insane," Lisa said as they wandered along the street, with large white houses rising up high on either side. "How much do you reckon they cost? Can you imagine ever having enough money?"

"They must be worth millions," he replied, checking the handwritten note Sasha had given him, showing the address for Elizabeth Barrington Stryke's home. "Tens of millions, even. We're definitely not in Crowford anymore." They walked along in silence for a moment, and Josh realized that Lisa was being uncharacteristically quiet. He glanced at her, waiting for her to start droning on about some TV show or comic book, and after a few more seconds he began to worry that something might be wrong. "You okay there?"

"Hmm? Oh, yeah. Fine."

They continued to walk, and now Josh felt more and more certain that she had something on her mind.

"It's crazy being possessed, right?" he said finally. "I keep looking back at last night and just... I can't quite believe it happened."

"Yeah. It's crazy."

"I think -"

"So are you and Sasha, like, ever going to be boyfriend and girlfriend?"

"No!" he spluttered. "I wish!"

"I bet you do."

"This isn't one of those situations where one person suddenly comes round and falls in love," he told her. "I just have to accept that my feelings for her will be unrequited forever. I'm sure over time I'll get over it, but until then it sucks. Have you ever had feelings for anyone?"

"Me?" She seemed shocked by the question for a moment. "No. I mean, yes. I mean... yes, I suppose so. I'm only human, right?"

"And how did it go?"

"Not terribly well," she admitted, glancing at him shyly before looking ahead again. "To be honest, I don't think he ever really quite realized that I liked him."

"Some oblivious moron?"

"You might say that."

"People like that are the worst," he told her, checking the note again before looking over at the nearest door. "Don't you want to just smack him round the head with a baseball bat and make him see sense? Or her, of course. I'm an open-minded guy."

"It's a he," she replied, "and yes, there are times when hitting him with a baseball bat feels very tempting. Then again, I guess I just have to accept that I'm not his type. You can't force stuff like that."

"You could try," he suggested. "Show him what he's missing."

"I don't think he's missing much, to be honest."

"Sure he is," he continued. "You're not so bad. Have a little more confidence. If you really like this guy, fight for him."

"This is a very confusing conversation," she replied. "So actually -"

"We're here," he said suddenly, stopping and looking up some steps toward a large blue door. "This is the house. It looks kind of scary, don't you think?"

She took a deep breath.

"So what's the plan?" she asked. "Are we just going to walk up there and ring the bell, and ask to talk to this Elizabeth woman?"

"She's going to want to talk to us when she finds out who we are," he replied, "and where we've come from today, and why we're here. Sasha thinks there has to be some bad blood, and she also thinks this woman might be sick. If that's the case, she might be much more willing to spill the beans. Not that we *want* her to be in a bad way, of course, but Sasha thinks this is our best bet. If Walter Stryke confessed what he'd done to anyone before he emigrated to Canada, I'm sure it'd be his wife."

"Okay," she said, forcing a smile, "I guess we should give it a try." She paused, before gesturing for him to step forward. "You're going to have to be the one who does all the talking, though," she told him. "I always get totally tongue-tied whenever I have to talk to rich people."

CHAPTER FOURTEEN

"WALTER," ELIZABETH SAID SOFTLY, after a moment of silence in the house's large and very airy drawing room. She paused, and for a moment tears seemed to fill her eyes. "I haven't thought of Walter Stryke for rather a long time."

"I'm sorry we just showed up here like this," Josh said. "We really wouldn't have disturbed you unless it was extremely important. As I explained to your butler, we're facing something of a race against time."

Glancing over her shoulder, Lisa saw the house's butler standing patiently by the door. She'd never seen an actual butler in the flesh before, and she couldn't help staring at him until – suddenly – he turned and looked directly at her. Startled, she smiled briefly before looking straight ahead.

"I have tried very hard," Elizabeth continued, "to put my time in Crowford in the past. I haven't been back there in more than forty years. I recall reading about the lifeboat tragedy when the Mercy Belle sank, but since then I have even managed to avoid reading any news about the place. As far as I am concerned, it's almost as if Crowford no longer exists."

"You might get your wish eventually," Josh replied, trying to make a joke. "The town's, uh... seen better days."

"I suppose I might as well ask this questions," she said to him, "even though I shouldn't care about the answer. Are those two repulsive Grace sisters still around?"

"You mean Angela and Vivian?" He nodded. "Yes, they're still alive."

"And are they still living in those two tiny little hovels?"

"The houses on Nelson Street?" He nodded again. "They're still there."

"Vivian Grace should have been locked away forever," Elizabeth murmured. "I have it on good authority that she did some truly awful things in the past that were covered up by her family. The fact that she ever got out of the hospital is an affront to modern decency."

"Well," Josh replied, "I think -"

"You know they have a tunnel connecting

their houses, don't you?" she added.

"I didn't know that, no," Josh said.

"Well, they do," she muttered. "I only know because I heard some gossip from someone who helped set the whole thing up. They act like they don't see one another, and I'm sure there's some bad blood between them, but they most certainly have a tunnel. I'm sure they meet down there occasionally, although I'm not sure what they could possibly have to talk about. Utterly wretched creatures, the pair of them."

"Your husband," Josh replied, hoping to steer the conversation back to the subject of Walter Stryke, "was rumored by some people to have been involved in the disappearance of a woman named Dorothy Maitland."

"Yes," Elizabeth said archly, "I recall that particular scandal. I saw the Maitland girl once and, well, she was certainly Walter's type. I wouldn't be at all surprised if he made advances when he was alone with her, he always had a taste for..." She paused, as if she was struggling to think of the right word. "He liked common girls. Uneducated. Foolish. Impressionable. Stupid is the word one might use."

"Are you saying that it was Dorothy Maitland's fault?" Lisa asked, clearly bristling at the older lady's words.

"I'm saying that it takes two to tango, my

dear," Elizabeth replied. "As for what happened to her, I can't possibly say, but let me assure you that Walter certainly had nothing to do with it. He might have liked feeling up the ladies, but murder? The man was a buffoon. He would never have been able to do something like that, or to cover it up. Ask anyone who knew him, he was a crumbling mess of a man. Even the slightest hint of his involvement was enough to turn him into a nervous wreck and send him scurrying off to the new world." She managed a derisory sniff. "I hope that makes things clear to you, and that you will end your investigations accordingly. I would take a very dim view if anyone tried to dredge up the past. You should thank your lucky stars that I deigned to explain this to you in person. Now please... get out of my sight and don't come back."

***

"Well, she was lovely," Lisa said as she and Josh made their way around the corner, heading back to the underground station. "Do you think she was born with that rod up her arse, or do you think it was inserted later in life?"

Josh turned to reply to her, but at that moment he spotted a familiar figure hurrying out from the back of Elizabeth's house and waving frantically. Stopping, he and Lisa watched as the butler navigated across a small park, clearly in a rush and desperate to avoid being seen.

"I'm so glad I managed to catch you," the man said breathlessly, stopping on the other side of the railing. He glanced back, as if he was terrified that he might be spotted. "I don't have long," he added, turning to them again, "but I heard what the old trout said to you in there and I wanted you to know something important. She was lying her face off. Or if not lying, then at least leaving a lot out."

"What do you mean?" Josh asked.

"She told me last week that she's letting me go soon," he explained, "so any loyalty I *might* have felt is gone. I've been with Lady Elizabeth for years, and my father was her butler before that, and she's treated us both abominably."

"Shocking," Lisa replied.

"My father worked for the family for decades," the butler continued, "including around the time when Walter Stryke emigrated to Canada. Or, rather, the time when he *supposedly* emigrated."

"Are you saying he didn't go?" Josh replied. "Was the whole thing faked?"

"Not quite," the butler explained. "Walter and his brother Oswald were twins, and Oswald died around the time that Dorothy Maitland disappeared. Now, my father was fed the same ridiculous story you just heard in there, but he was an observant man and he always swore that a switch had been made. The man who emigrated to Canada was Oswald, not Walter."

"Why would they cover that up?" Lisa asked.

"They had to explain why one brother was gone," the man told her. "My father could never be sure, but he believed that Walter Stryke disappeared on the same night that the Maitland woman went missing."

"Are you sure?" Josh replied.

"As sure as I can be. Walter disappeared, and Oswald showed up to clean up the mess. For whatever reason, he assumed his brother's identity and promptly headed across the Atlantic. Meanwhile a story was concocted, claiming that Oswald had died in London. People were so busy pointing fingers at the man they believed had something to do with Dorothy Maitland's disappearance, they didn't have time to look too deeply into the stories about Oswald." He looked over his shoulder again. "I can't prove it," he added finally, "but I've always believed that my father was right. Whatever happened to Walter Stryke, he was never seen again after that night at the department store."

"What about Dorothy Maitland?" Josh asked. "Do you have any idea what happened to her?"

"I'm sorry, I don't," the man said, taking a

step back. "I've been out here for too long already, but you have to believe me, a lot of people worked very hard to keep the truth from coming out. Do you really think a woman like Lady Elizabeth would entertain two young strangers who show up at her door asking questions? Of course she wouldn't, not unless she was desperate to make sure that the truth remained hidden forever. She's the last surviving member of the Stryke family, but she won't want their name getting dragged through the mud."

"That explains why we were both possessed," Josh said, turning to Lisa. "There are two ghosts there, one's Dorothy Maitland and the other's Walter Stryke."

"My head's spinning," she admitted.

"That's all I know," the butler said, turning and heading back toward the rear of the house. "Don't tell anyone that you talked to me! At least, not until next Friday. That's my last day, after that I don't give a damn!" Walking away, he held up his right hand and raised the middle digit. "Believe me, I'm looking forward to tell Lady Elizabeth exactly what I think or her and her stinking family."

"This mystery is getting murkier and murkier," Josh said, turning to Lisa once again. "I'm no closer to understanding what really happened at Stryke Brothers forty-nine years ago. In fact, I almost feel like I understand less now that I know

Walter Stryke might have died that night."

"I've got a feeling we've been looking for answers in the wrong place," she told him. "Hey, do you happen to know when Tommo's got his next late shift at the supermarket?"

CHAPTER FIFTEEN

"I DON'T MIND TELLING you guys," Tommo said, standing in the fruit and veg aisle with a mop in his hands and a bucket at his feet, "that I've got a terrible no-good absolutely awful feeling about this idea."

"Relax," Josh said with a sigh, "how many times do I have to tell you? We just want to look around."

"For what?"

"If we knew that, we wouldn't have to look," he pointed out. "We just think there might be something here, something that could illuminate our search."

"It's a stab in the dark," Lisa added. "Speaking of which, is there any way you could turn the lights off."

"The lights?" Tommo replied. "In the entire supermarket?"

"We're the only ones here, aren't we?" she reminded him. "You said it yourself, they're far too cheap to pay for anyone to help you clean up after closing time, so you're left here to do it. That's the only thing you talk about when you're drunk."

"It is?"

She and Josh both nodded.

"Well, I've got a point," Tommo continued. "You know, technically I could put in a complaint, but then I'd just get fired and for better or worse I need this job right now. Besides, the joke's on them, because I do an absolutely atrocious job. To be honest, most of the time I just sweep all the junk under the shelves and leave it to fester."

"You seem almost proud of that approach," Josh suggested.

"Damn straight!" he replied, clenching a fist and bumping his own chest, directly over his heart. "I take the man's coin, but there's no way I'm displaying anything more than the most basic level of competence. You pay minimum wage, you get minimum effort. They need to learn that. Well, they don't actually pay minimum wage yet, but if that ever comes into force, I'll adjust my mindset accordingly."

"Right," Josh said, glancing awkwardly at Lisa for a moment before turning to Tommo again.

"We just want to take a look around. This might be a complete waste of time, but you never know, something might jump out at us. We have to try, at least."

"Do what you want," Tommo replied, before pushing the mop's head into the water and then starting to clean around the display of potatoes. "The light-switches are by the door behind you, turn them off if you need to. It's not like it'll change my job too much. Just make sure you're done by midnight, okay? Because that's when I'm out of here."

***

"I'm not sure his approach to cleaning really works," Josh said a short while later, as he and Lisa made their way along the darkened tea and coffee aisle, with only two flashlights to guide their way. "Have you seen all the dust on the floor?"

"I suppose the bosses don't really care," Lisa replied, before falling silent for a moment. "I get the feeling that attention to detail isn't really their thing."

"So what exactly are we looking for?" Josh asked. "We already checked the stock area near the back door, and there was nothing. I don't mean to sound skeptical, but I've been to this supermarket loads of times before and I've never once spotted anything out of the ordinary. Why should that change tonight?"

"Beats me," she said, glancing at him with a faint smile, "but you're right, last night while I was possessed by Dorothy Maitland I was frantically trying to get in here. That makes me think that on that awful night back in 1949, when she was running from Walter Stryke, she ended up for some reason in the old bombed-out church."

"And then what?"

"Your guess is as good as mine," she said as they reached the end of the aisle and looked around, before heading down the cereal aisle. She aimed her flashlight straight ahead. "My optimistic side thinks Dorothy was trying to use me to show us something. My pessimistic side, meanwhile, wonders whether she's just trapped in a loop, and she wasn't trying to show us anything."

"Why do you care?" he asked.

"What do you mean?"

"I'm here because I want to find out why that ghost attacked Sasha," he reminded her, "and Sasha was just driven by curiosity. But I don't get why you're so invested in trying to solve this mystery."

"Well," she said cautiously, clearly struggling to come up with an answer, "I suppose I'm just... curious."

"You're still going to a lot of effort."

"Do you want me to stop?"

"No, not at all," he replied. "I mean, you can if you want, but I just thought it was odd, that's all. It's not like you get anything out of this."

"True," she admitted, before stopping as she looked down once more at the floor. "Hey, do you notice anything here?"

Looking down, he paused for a moment as he glanced around.

"Anything at all?" Lisa continued.

"Am I missing something?"

"Where's the dirt?" she asked. "Tommo just sweeps it under the shelves, and as we've seen already it kind of lingers and you can see it. But along this side..."

She pointed to one side of the aisle, aiming her flashlight's beam at the floor, where the space under the shelving was surprisingly clean.

"There's nothing," she added. "See?"

"So?" he replied with a shrug. "He probably just did a better job in this section."

"A truly laughable idea," she said, before getting down onto her hands and knees and peering under the shelf. "I don't see any dust bunnies," she continued, "or anything much at all." Squinting, she tried to see a little better as she shone the flashlight's beam into the narrow space. After a moment, she saw a dark space on the floor, as well as some cracks. "There's *something* here, though.

It's like a small gap in the floor, and I think it runs under most of this section of shelving."

"Does that really help us?" he asked. "This place is a few decades old, I'm sure it's completely falling apart, and I bet they don't spend much on maintenance. I mean, they hire Tommo to keep it clean, so clearly they're not too fussed."

"Does this shelf move?" she replied, getting to her feet again.

"The entire shelf? Are you crazy?"

"We need to see what's under there," she told him. "Come on, we went to all this trouble, we can't just back down now." She pushed against the nearest shelf. "I can feel some give in it," she continued. "I don't think it's bolted into place, so we should be able to shift it aside."

"I'm not sure we should start reorganizing the supermarket."

"We'll put it back," she told him, before gesturing for him to join her. "It only needs to move aside by a few feet so we can get a better look at what's down there." She waited, and then she gestured again. "Why am I the one who's having to do the persuading here? This started out as your project, so put some muscle behind it."

"Fine," he replied, getting into position, "but I don't really think we're going to have much luck with this. It's an entire supermarket shelving unit, and it's got loads of packets of cereal on it. We're not going to -"

Suddenly the shelves jerked slightly as Lisa started pushing. Realizing that he needed to get stuck in, Josh began to push as well, and to his surprise they were slowly but surely able to start sliding the unit across the floor. Feeling a little breathless, Josh had to adjust his grip several times, but he knew he couldn't give up and after a moment his foot began to dip into a deep crack in the floor.

"Keep going!" Lisa hissed as the shelves' legs scraped loudly. "We're almost there!"

"What are you guys doing?" Tommo shouted for one of the other aisles. "What the hell is that noise?"

Letting out a loud gasp, Lisa finally stepped back; Josh followed, and they both quickly saw that with the shelves out of the way, a large crack had been exposed in the floor, revealing what appeared to be a substantial gap that led deep beneath the supermarket itself. For a moment, neither of them really knew what to say, and they could only stare down at the hole as Tommo began to make his way along the aisle.

"Well," Lisa said finally, raising both eyebrows, "at least now we know why there was no dirt under this particular set of shelves. It must have all fallen down there." She paused for a moment. "Wherever *there* turns out to be."

CHAPTER SIXTEEN

"IT'S DEEP," JOSH SAID a couple of minutes later, kneeling on the floor with his right arm reaching deep into the crack. "I can't feel the bottom at all. It's cold, too."

"You guys need to put these shelves back immediately," Tommo said firmly. "If someone sees this damage, I'll be fired!"

"We didn't *make* the hole," Josh said, pulling his arm out and then trying once more to shine the flashlight's beam into the gap, only to see more darkness. "It was here already. It's probably been here for a while. If anything, the supermarket should be grateful to us for revealing what seems to be some kind of serious structural problem. I don't know when this thing opened up, but it must have been after the last time the shelves were moved."

"The tiles are bulging up," Lisa pointed out. "I don't think this is collapsing, I think something's pushing up from underground." She turned to Tommo. "Is there a basement or anything else under the supermarket?"

"Not that I've ever heard of," he replied. "I'm pretty sure I'd have heard. I mean, there must be foundations and stuff like that, but all the storage areas are out the back."

"It looks loose," Lisa continued, kneeling next to Josh and grabbing the edge of the crack, then pulling on the broken tiles and immediately pulling some away. "Look!"

"Stop that!" Tommo hissed. "Do you have any idea how much trouble you're going to get me into?"

"That should be enough," Lisa said, setting one of the broken sections aside.

"Enough for what?" Josh asked.

"What do you think?" she replied, turning to him with a faintly nervous smile. "This *has* to be connected to Dorothy Maitland and whatever happened to us back in the shoe shop. If we go to the supermarket's manager, or to the police, everything'll slow to a crawl and we might never find out what's going on." She looked back down into the hole, which was now a fair bit larger. "Relax," she added, "I'm not expecting either of you guys to go in. I'll do it."

"In?" Josh replied, puzzled for a moment before realizing what she meant. "Are you insane? There's no way I'm letting you do that!"

"And there's no way I'm letting you stop me," she countered. "Besides, it's completely safe. I've got you two big strong guys to look after me."

"You can't just jump into some random hole in the ground," Josh said firmly. "You have no idea what's down there!"

"It can't be *that* deep," she told him, "and I'm not going to just leap blindly into it." She fumbled in her pockets for a moment, before pulling out a 2p coin. "I'll drop this down and we'll be able to hear when it hits the bottom." Reaching into the crack, she let go of the coin, which fell into the darkness and disappeared. They all waited, but they heard nothing. "That doesn't mean it's dangerous," Lisa added, although she seemed a little uncertain now. "It probably just landed on dirt."

"Or this is a bottomless pit," Tommo suggested.

Josh and Lisa both turned to him.

"I don't like this one bit," he continued. "My dudes, what started out as a bit of fun has rapidly become much more serious. For all we know, this means the structural integrity of the entire supermarket is open to question. If you could down there, you might trip or nudge something, and then the whole building could start to fall down on top of us."

"That's a fair point," Lisa admitted.

"Or there could be pipes," he added, "even gas pipes, and if you dislodge one then the place could explode. Or there could be rats and you'll be attacked, or there might genuinely be a really big drop and you'll fall down and we won't be able to get to you in time. If that's not enough, I'm sure I can think of at least a hundred more reasons why we totally need to hold back and not do anything stupid. Let's not Famous Five this shit."

"You're totally right," Lisa replied.

"Thank you," he said with a relieved sigh. "You know, it's actually really cool that people are listening to me for once. I'm so used to being ignored, I can't even remember the last time anyone took my comments seriously."

He waited for them to agree with him and start moving the shelves back into place, but after a few seconds he realized that they were both simply staring at him as if they were waiting for some other cue.

"What?" he asked finally.

"We're going down into the hole," Josh and Lisa both said at the same time.

***

"Do you see anything?" Josh asked, holding Lisa's

hand tight as she disappeared fully into the space beneath the supermarket's floor. "Do you feel anything? Lisa, are you okay?"

"Hang on!" she called up to him. "I'm just getting my bearings."

"I think this is the wrong approach," he continued. "Lisa, come back up and I'll go down instead."

"We discussed this already," she reminded him, pulling her hand free as she clambered deeper into the hole. "I'm smaller than you, I'm more likely to fit. Just give me a moment to take a look around and then I'll tell you what I see."

"But -"

"Plus there are a *lot* of spiders," she added. "I've seen a dozen already, at least. You're not a big fan of spiders, Josh, are you?"

"No," he said awkwardly. "No, I'm not."

"Wimp," Tommo murmured, having knelt next to him on the floor.

"You could always go instead," Josh told him.

"With these hips?" Tommo replied. "I once got stuck in the seat of a zombie shoot 'em up game at an arcade in Broadstairs."

"Whatever," Josh said, peering down into the hole for a moment longer before turning to him again. "Seriously?"

Tommo shrugged.

"I don't see a lot!" Lisa called up to them, already sounding much deeper. "It's pretty narrow down here, and there are lots of old roots growing through the mud!"

"If there's nothing there, you should come back!" Josh shouted.

"I still can't tell if it leads anywhere," she explained. "I don't know, I think it sort of opens up a little more near the bottom. Or further down, at least. I'm really not sure where the bottom is. This thing's much deeper than I expected."

"I don't like this," Josh said after a moment. "What if she just vanishes and we never hear from her again? What if she falls and breaks something? How are we going to explain to the police what we were doing here in the first place?"

"What if she finds buried treasure," Tommo replied, "and we split it three ways, and we're all rich beyond our wildest dreams."

"That seems unlikely."

"But not impossible," Tommo continued. "You've got to be ready for whatever life throws at you, because if you don't grab the chance when it arrives, someone else will. Sure, there's probably not a pirate galleon or a treasure chest or a crashed alien spaceship down there, but what if there is? How would you handle it?"

"You're crazy," Josh replied. "You realize that, right? You're absolutely crazy."

"I don't like that term very much," Tommo told him. "In fact -"

Before he could finish, they both heard a bumping sound coming from one of the other aisles. They looked over their shoulders, and after a few seconds Tommo got to his feet.

"It was probably nothing," Josh whispered.

"Or it was my manager coming back for something," Tommo suggested, his voice filled with a sudden sense of panic. "Wait right here and try not to lose Lisa down there. I'm just going to check and make sure we don't have company." He made his way toward the end of the aisle, before disappearing around the corner. "If Rona's come back for something and catches us doing this, she'll have me out the door before I even have a chance to apologize."

"Are you okay down there?" Josh called out after a moment, leaning closer to the crack again. "Don't worry, there was a bit of a noise up here, but I'm sure it was nothing. This place is probably infested with rats, I wouldn't be surprised if they're as big as dogs by now. I hope Tommo took something he can use to defend himself."

He paused for a moment, waiting for a reply, before shining his flashlight down into the darkness.

"Lisa?"

He waited, but with each passing second he felt a growing rush of fear in his chest.

"Lisa?" he called out, trying not to panic. "Why aren't you saying anything? Can you hear me? Lisa, say something!"

CHAPTER SEVENTEEN

"HELLO?" TOMMO WHISPERED CAUTIOUSLY, stepping around another corner and looking along the bread, eggs and baking aisle. "Is anyone here?"

With the lights still off, he could barely see anything at all, even as he raised his flashlight and cast the beam toward the far end. He'd been trying to convince himself that the sound he'd heard earlier had been nothing, that the supermarket was just 'settling' like an old house in a more conventional horror story, but his fears weren't quite gone just yet. In fact, as he began to accept that perhaps there were no ghosts in the supermarket after all, he became more worried that his manager might have shown up.

"Hey, Rona," he continued, as he began to

make his way along the aisle, "if you're here, I know you probably think that this whole situations is a little weird. And it is, if I'm honest, but I can explain everything if you just give me a chance. When you hear me out, I'm convinced you'll agree that this totally isn't a firing offense. I know you have the three strikes policy, but the old strikes have to fall out of consideration eventually, don't they?"

Reaching the mid-section of the aisle, he looked both ways along the central passage and still saw no sign of anyone or anything. He raised the flashlight and picked out the ends of various aisles, and he reasoned that Rona would certainly have made her presence known by now, most likely by yelling at the top of her voice. In that case, however, his thoughts began to drift back to his other worry.

Ghosts.

"There's no such thing as a haunted supermarket," he muttered under his breath. "The idea's completely ludicrous. A haunted supermarket's about as likely as a haunted... shoe shop. Or coffee shop." He swallowed hard. "Okay, those probably weren't the best examples right now, but the point still stands." He turned and shone the flashlight in the other direction, just to reassure himself that there was no-one else around. "What kind of ghost would even be seen dead in a place like this, anyway?"

As those words left his lips, he was entirely

unaware that the spectral figure of the long-dead Walter Stryke was standing directly behind him, glaring in the darkness at the back of his head.

***

"Damn it!" Lisa hissed, dropping down to the muddy bottom of the hole in the supermarket's floor and, in the process, dropping her flashlight. "Great."

Reaching down, she picked the flashlight up and shone it straight ahead. The gap leading down from the shop floor above had narrowed a lot before, at the last moment, widening again and allowing her to jump to the bottom. Looking up, she was unable to see the opening; the wall curved slightly, but she told herself that she'd be able to climb up again easily enough. She estimated that she was probably thirty or forty feet below ground level, which was much further than she'd expected to get. Tree roots criss-crossed the space, but they were easy enough to break away, and despite the cold damp air she wasn't too worried.

"Josh?" she called out. "Can you hear me up there?"

"Lisa!" he shouted, his voice barely audible. "Are you okay?"

"Yeah, I just had to concentrate for a few minutes!" she yelled. "It's kind of hard to talk and climb at the same time. At least, it is if you're me

AMY CROSS

and you're not used to it, and you don't want to fall!"

"Where are you?" he shouted.

"At the bottom!" she told him. "Just wait a moment and let me take a look round, okay?"

She heard him shouting again, but this time she lacked the patience to keep saying the same thing over and over again. Instead she began to inch her way along what seemed to be a long, narrow corridor cut into the ground; reaching out, she touched the muddy wall, and she realized that this was less of a corridor and more of a natural fissure that seemed to have opened up at some point in the past. A moment later her right foot bumped against something, and she looked down to see what appeared to be some pieces of masonry.

She picked up one of the pieces and turned it around, and she realized that it reminded her of one thing in particular.

"A church," she whispered, before looking up again as the pieces began to come together in her thoughts. "A bomb landed on the old church and destroyed it. This hole in the ground must have been opened up."

She thought for a moment of a bomb exploding high above, blasting the church to pieces. She'd heard a few times about that happening, and when she looked at the chunk of stone in her hand again she realized that a few pieces of the church must have collapsed into the resulting crater, which in turn she supposed was where she stood now. From what she remembered, the ruins of the church had stood for a number of years after the war until the local council took the controversial decision to sell the site instead of rebuilding what had been there previously; the supermarket company had promised to excavate fully, but she had no trouble believing that they hadn't kept to their word.

"Wonderful," she said, setting the piece of stone down and setting off again through the gap into ground, having to walk slightly sideways in an attempt to keep from rubbing against the uneven sides. "No wonder the building above is starting to crumble, there's no -"

Suddenly she heard a gasping sound. Spinning round, she shone her flashlight back the way she'd just come; she saw no sign of anyone, but the gasping sound – which had faded now – had seemed very real and very close, as if someone had been struggling to breathe just a few feet away.

"Hello?" she called out, a little unnerved by the sound of fear in her own voice. "Is someone else down here?"

She waited, telling herself that of course there was no-one else nearby, yet the more she replayed the sound in her head, the more certain she felt that it had been an actual person. Or, at least, something that had *once* been an actual person.

"I'm only trying to help," she continued, as the bulb in her flashlight began to flicker. "My name's Lisa and if you can hear me, I came down here because..."

Her voice trailed off as she tried to work out exactly why she was currently standing in a deep trench several feet beneath the floor of Benson's.

"I came down here because if you're not at rest," she explained, "I'd like to fix that. I have no idea what it's like to be trapped like this, endlessly repeating your own death, never able to get any peace. I think you might be reaching out and asking for someone to help you, so if that's what you'd like, just tell me what you need."

The flashlight flickered again, as if it was starting to die.

"Don't you dare," Lisa whispered, looking down at the device in her hand. "Don't even think about -"

Before she could finish, the flashlight fell dark. She gave it a quick shake, but she already knew that she only had one option. Reaching into her pocket, she fumbled around for a moment, trying to find the spare batteries she'd brought along; once they were in her hand, she opened the flashlight to take out the dead batteries, but as she worked she realized she could hear the gasping sound, as if something was moving closer through the darkness. Now she was starting to panic a little, and as she pulled the old batteries out she managed to drop everything.

"Damn it!" she snapped, falling down onto her knees and reaching around, unable to see a thing.

As the gasping sound continued, she found the flashlight itself and then all four batteries. Not knowing which battery was which, however, she had to try them two at a time, even as the gasps began to fill her ears.

"Come on, please," she stammered, trying yet another combination only to find that nothing seemed to be working. "I swear I'll be a better person, I'll go to church and everything, but please just get me out of here. I'm not -"

In that instant the flashlight burst back to life. The gasping sound stopped abruptly as Lisa aimed the beam straight ahead, and to her relief she once again saw nothing. A fraction of a second later, however, she heard the gasping sound again, this time coming from over her shoulder. She began to turn, only to see a pale hand touching the top of her arm from behind. Holding her breath, she turned all the way, and to her horror she saw a rotten female face glaring at her.

"No!" Lisa screamed stumbling away and starting to race along the passageway, before frantically climbing up the wall, using the roots to support herself. "Josh, help me!" she shouted.

"There's something down here! Josh!"

Spotting the entrance to the hole up ahead, she saw Josh's shocked face staring back down at her. She began to look down, only to lose her grip on the flashlight once more, letting it tumble back down. For a fraction of a second she saw the rotten women climbing up after her, and she immediately began to haul her way up again, following a different route to the one she'd taken on her way down. And then, as she grabbed another thick set of roots, she froze as she saw a skeletal human figure entangled so deeply in the roots that she's almost missed them entirely.

"Lisa?" Josh called out. "Lisa, say something! What's wrong?"

CHAPTER EIGHTEEN

"AND HERE'S THE LAST piece," Detective Marshall said the following morning, setting the cracked human skull down on a stretch of tarpaulin that had been laid out across the aisle to hold the various bones. "The most important of all, one might say."

"Did you get all of it?" Lisa asked, her voice trembling with fear. "You can't leave any part of her down there."

"We got it all," Marshall replied, turning to her. "We'll have to send it off for formal identification, but Doctor Lewis says it's female and that the condition of the bones is in line with it having been down there for a number of decades."

"So it's Dorothy Maitland, right?" Josh said. "It has to be!"

"It doesn't *have* to be anything," Marshall told him, clearly unimpressed, "although the odds certainly seem high."

"What about the woman at the bottom?" Lisa asked. "Did you find that too?"

"I've had two guys down there checking it out," he replied. "They've covered the entire space and reported no sign of any..." He took a moment to check his notes again. "Rotten zombie-like screaming corpses with a lust for blood."

"That's what I saw!" Lisa snapped.

"They found your flashlight," he added, holding it up for her to see. "It'll be processed and, so long as the supermarket doesn't change its mind and press charges, it'll be returned to you in due course."

"What could they even charge us with?" Josh asked. "We didn't break in. We didn't cause any of this damage. We actually helped them!"

"I'm not sure they agree," Marshall told him, "but they're also in damage limitation mode and they don't want to cause any ill-feeling in the local community. You should thank your lucky stars for that, because otherwise you might be sitting in a cell right now contemplating charges relating to trespass and other very serious matters."

"They didn't even know the hole was there," Josh pointed out. "It's obvious that something was trying to force its way up. That was probably the ghost of Dorothy Maitland trying to get someone to find her bones after all these years. I just hope she can rest in peace now."

"Me too," Lisa added, looking over at the hole in the floor. "I really don't want to ever run into her again."

"That seems unlikely," Marshall told her, "because I spoke to the supermarket's manager just now, and although there'll be no charges, she was very clear on one matter. You two are barred from ever setting foot in this supermarket ever again. And if you even come within twenty feet of the front door, I'll be dragging you away so fast you won't know what hit you."

***

"Rona fired me," Tommo said as the three of them sat in the coffee shop a few hours later, feeling very sorry for themselves. "Apparently it wasn't even under the three strikes policy. My actions last night, according to her, added up to a whole load of strikes on their own."

"The important thing," Josh said after a moment, "is that we helped Dorothy Maitland find peace at last. The police are going to track down her closest living relatives, wherever they might live now, and make sure that she's given a proper burial."

"Imagine spending five decades trapped in the darkness," Lisa added, clearly still reliving her experience down in the hole. "Imagine experiencing the night of your death over and over again, as part of some desperate attempt to get help from the living. She might have been going through her own private version of Hell." She paused for a moment, before looking over at Josh. "What about Walter Stryke?"

"We can't solve everything," he told her. "The police said they didn't find more bodies down there."

"So he just gets away with killing her?"

"The man's dead," Josh replied, "so whether he got away with it very much comes down to your personal beliefs. If you're anything like me, you might believe that in the next life he had to pay for what he'd done."

"But his ghost possessed you," she pointed out. "Dorothy possessed me, and Walter possessed you. Doesn't that seem like a loose end?"

"I'm tired," Josh said, getting to his feet, "and I'm about to start a new shift, so I'm not going to be able to sit down again for another nine hours." Stepping past her, he stopped to put a hand on her shoulder. "Consider this case closed," he added. "We got to do some pretty cool stuff in the process. I can't wait to get to the hospital tomorrow morning and tell Sasha all about it, she's going to be so relieved."

Lisa and Tommo sat in silence for a moment as Josh walked away.

"Sasha this," Lisa said finally, "and Sasha that. Sometimes I think he's completely under her thumb."

"Do I detect jealousy?" Tommo asked with a faint smile. "I think I detect jealousy!"

"As if," he murmured, before turning and watching as Josh slipped into his apron. "Maybe before," she added, "but there's no way I can compete with Sasha. She's smart and fun and funny, and I'm just... me."

"You just solved a pretty major mystery," Tommo reminded her.

"That's nothing," she muttered. "He's still head over heels in love with Sasha, and nothing's going to change that." She hauled herself up from the chair. "I know when I'm beaten. I'm just going to go home and watch something and generally pig out for the rest of the day."

"Want some company?" he asked.

"Nah, I'm good," she replied as she headed to the door. "I think I just want to be alone so I can get my head around all the crazy stuff that's been happening."

"I know the feeling," Tommo said, finishing the last of his tea before standing and wandering over to the counter, where Josh was busy organizing some mugs. "So," he continued, "what now? If the coffee shop's no longer haunted, doesn't that kind of make it a little... boring?"

"Al's is on its last legs," Josh told him, "and from what I heard, after the end of the month the old shoe shop next door is just going to become another vacant store in this dying town. The days of Stryke Brothers and other flash shops are long over, now it's just going to be an endless parade of charity shops and low-market dumps." He began to load the dishwasher. "I don't know about you, but I'm seriously going to start thinking about how to get out of Crowford. I don't want this town dragging me down with it. Even if I only get as far as Canterbury, I'm determined to break free."

"You and me both," Tommo admitted. "I'm going to take this as a sign that I need to make a change. And now if you'll excuse me, I'm off to check the noticeboards to see what's going." He turned and headed toward the door. "Something tells me I won't get a glowing reference from Rona."

"Glad to see you're working hard for a change," Betty said as she stopped to watch Josh putting another load into the dishwasher. "You haven't been pulling your weight lately."

"That's all going to change," he replied with a force smile. "Don't worry, Betty. From now on, for as long as I'm here, I'll be the best employee Al's ever had."

"I'll settle for tolerable," she replied as she wandered over to the till to serve another customer. "Tolerable's enough."

"But don't get used to it," Josh continued, as he set some more mugs into the machine. "Tommo's right, everything that's been happening lately is a clear sign that we've hit the end of the road in this town." He moved the mugs around for a moment, trying to fit some more into the tray, and then he paused for a moment, staring into the cavernous metallic space in the rear of the machine. "I'm going to sign up for college in September, and I'm going to study hard and then I'm going to get out of here, and then one day I'll be rich and successful somewhere far from here. Sasha's bound to like me then, and I won't have to care about anyone else."

He shut the machine and set it on, and then he headed through to the storeroom at the back of the shop.

"This time," he added, "I won't let anything or anyone stop me."

As he disappeared into the back, he bumped against the communal noticeboard above the condiments. High up on that noticeboard, an A4 poster was advertising bright and exciting college courses for anyone who wanted to start studying in September 1998.

AMY CROSS

CHAPTER NINETEEN

SEVERAL MONTHS LATER, THE same noticeboard displayed a new poster, advertising a set of brand new college courses that would be starting in September 1999.

"Don't forget to clean the nozzle on the hot water kettle this time," Betty said as she slipped her arms into her jacket. "We've had three people almost throwing up today, and I'm convinced that nozzle's to blame. You know, come to think of it, I don't remember a single time since I started here when that nozzle *ever* got cleaned."

"I'll do it," Josh replied as he finished re-stacking the selection of teabags. "You don't have to keep reminding me."

"Evidently I do," she said as she headed to the door. "I'll be inspecting it in the morning!"

"Mind you don't take your eye out," Josh said, glancing over his shoulder and watching as she walked outside. Hurrying over, he slid the bolt across to make sure that no more customers arrived, and then he checked his watch. Sure, he was closing a few minutes early, but he figured he'd earned that right after a busy day filled with a succession of loud customers and their screaming children.

Looking out at the street, he saw that rain was starting to fall, tapping gently at the puddles. The sun had set a little earlier, and the sight of Crowford High Street on a rainy Wednesday evening left Josh feeling utterly dispirited as he headed past the counter and through to the storeroom.

"This is *definitely* going to be my last year here," he told himself. "As soon as Gran's out of the hospital and I've set her up with a home-care assistant, I'm going to sign up to one of those courses."

***

"It's brilliant!" Tommo gasped, struggling to contain his excitement as he stood at the bar in Nelson's. "Seriously, I'd recommend it to anyone. Plus, Reading's not even that far from London, so I get to go to all the gigs I want."

"But you miss Crowford just a little bit,

don't you?" Lisa replied with a smile. "Come on, admit it, you have to miss the local bands, at least."

"Doesn't look like much has changed to me," Tommo said, glancing around. "All the same old faces drinking the same old drinks, just with gravity having done a bit more of a number of on their faces. Honestly, Lisa, coming back just reminds me why I was right to leave." He turned to her again. "What about you? Any plans?"

"I'm thinking about it," she told him. "I just want to make sure I make the right choice."

"What about Josh?" he asked. "I've sent him a few messages but he didn't get back to me. Is he still working at the coffee shop?"

"I think so," she said, somewhat evasively. "I don't really know. I've spotted him out and about once or twice."

"You know, I dine out on that story at uni," Tommo continued. "I exaggerate my involvement a little bit, so that I'm not the comedy sidekick, but people think it's pretty cool that I helped discover a dead body hidden under the floor of a supermarket. I've even saved a clipping from the paper to prove what happened, because some people think the story's too ridiculous."

"They're not the only ones," she admitted, as the band on the stage began to warm up.

"I see Josh didn't get lucky in love," Tommo said, looking past her.

Turning, Lisa saw Sasha kissing a guy over by the door to the toilets.

"He's about the only person she *hasn't* been out with," she murmured. "She was dating Doug Williams before that, and Sally Hansfield before that, and I think it was Mark Durgan back in the summer."

"She's into girls now?"

"She's into everyone," she explained. "I mean, all power to her, but her relationships never last long and she's always overlapping them, if you know what I mean."

"Sounds like Josh got a lucky escape. He's not *still* pining for her, is he?"

"I really couldn't tell you. Like I said, I haven't spoken to him for a very long time. If I'm completely honest, I've been kind of avoiding him. I don't even walk past the coffee shop unless I have to, just in case I bump into him. I know he's not interested in me, and I'm trying to force myself to just think about something – anything – else." She paused for a few seconds. "I'll get there eventually."

"Sasha clearly gets around," Tommo observed. "I suppose she's celebrating life, after almost getting killed a while back when something threw her down the stairs. Maybe when she's dated every single other person in Crowford, Josh'll get his turn."

"Maybe," Lisa said, before spotting an older

man watching her from near the bar. She met his gaze, and although she knew she recognized him from somewhere, she couldn't quite place him. A moment later, feeling a little uncomfortable, she turned to Tommo again just as the band began their first song. "Right," she continued, forcing a smile. "Did anyone in Reading get around to teaching you how to dance?"

***

The brightly-lit sign outside Al's flickered slightly in the rain before suddenly switching off. Below, Josh peered out through the rain-spattered window, checking that the sign was dark before turning and heading back across the coffee shop.

"Boring," he said with a heavy sigh as he checked his watch. "Boring, boring, boring."

Stopping next to the wall, he saw the same swirly patterns that had been there since the shop's most recent refit. He took a deep breath, and he thought back to the days when Sasha had been working next door, to their regular late-night Wednesday meet-ups on the fire escape. Feeling more than a little nostalgic, he finally reached out and knocked on the door, the way he always had in the old days back when Sasha had been at the shoe shop, back when there had even *been* a shoe shop. The unit next to Al's had been empty for months.

Turning, he walked over to the counter.

Suddenly he heard a loud, muffled knock. Looking over his shoulder, he saw the wall again; he knew that the shop next door had been locked and left abandoned for ages, yet there was no doubting the fact that someone had just knocked on the other side of the wall.

Stepping back over, Josh stared at the wall for a few seconds before knocking again. He waited, and this time he heard something else; leaning closer, he put an ear to the wall and listened, and he realized he could hear a scratching sound coming from the other side, as if someone in the dark and shuttered old shoe shop was running their fingernails against the wallpaper.

"What the..."

As the sound faded to nothing, Josh pulled back and stared at the wall once more.

"I'm really not in the mood for this," he murmured, thinking back to the days when he and Sasha had discussed ghost stories. He checked his watch and saw that the delivery wasn't due for some time yet, and then he looked up at the ceiling and saw the bulge where the shop's interior had been forced to accommodate part of the old Stryke Brothers building. "We fixed the ghost problem here, remember?" he continued. "We had to dig up the supermarket floor to do it, but I'm pretty sure no-one else has died here since, so there really can't be any new ghosts."

He waited, hearing only silence.

"And the old ones are long gone," he added. "Dorothy Maitland was given a proper burial. Her bones are six feet under, in a cemetery a long way from here. Somewhere near Paddock Wood, I think, where her relatives live. So I'm afraid, spooky noise, that you don't scare me."

In an attempt to prove that point, he knocked once again on the wall, a little louder this time. He thought of the dark and empty old shoe shop next door; he knew that all the shelves and other items had been removed a long time ago, leaving only the shell of what had been there before. The windows had been boarded up after a bunch of local kids had smashed the glass, so he figured that the interior of the actual shoe shop had been left completely untouched for ages, which in itself would have been a spooky thought if he didn't know with absolute certainty that any ghosts were long gone.

"Okay, then," he said out loud, "time to -"

Suddenly he heard footsteps ringing out in the distance, marching toward the other side of the wall. He only had time to start to open his mouth again, before a ghostly figure stepped straight through from the shop next door and passed through Josh's body, sending him crumpling to the floor.

AMY CROSS

CHAPTER TWENTY

"AND WHEN I RIP my way out of the Devil's gut, I'll make sure I spit on his face on my way up!"

"These lyrics are terrible," Lisa said, wincing as she turned to Tommo. "I'm going to the bar to get another drink. Want one?"

"And some earplugs, if they have them," he replied. "Oh, and maybe a tranquilizer gun with four darts? I reckon I could take out the entire band from this spot."

Smiling, Lisa squeezed her way through the surprisingly large crowd that had gathered to witness the final act of the night. Of course, for Crowford a surprisingly large crowd was only fifty or so people, but Lisa was still impressed by the town's desire for punishment as she finally reached the bar and signaled to Evan for the same drinks again. Feeling as if she'd just emerged from a mosh pit, she leaned against a rare dry part of the bar and tried to regain her equilibrium, although after a few seconds she heard angry yelling nearby. She turned just in time to see Sasha screaming at some guy and then storming out of the club.

Looking back at the bar, she realized that she was being watched. She waited for the sensation to pass, and then she oh-so-casually looked to her left and saw the older guy from earlier staring at her. This time, he was too close and his glare was too insistent for her to ignore; sure enough, after a few seconds he made his way over, and Lisa could already tell from his slightly glassy eyes that the whiskey in his hand was not his first of the night.

"You don't recognize me, do you?" he said, slurring his words slightly.

"Sorry, I -"

"Jake," he continued, holding a hand out for her to shake. "Marshall. People call me Jake."

"Hi, Jake," she replied, shaking his hand even though it was slightly cold and wet. "Having a fun night?"

"You still don't recognize me."

"Sorry," she said, relieved that Evan was bringing her drinks over. She pulled a note from her pocket and handed it to him. "Well, have a -"

"The supermarket," he said, before she could finish. "The hole in the floor? The one you and your fellow Scooby gang members got all excited about?"

"Right," she said, surprised to realize that this was in fact the police detective who'd dealt with the situation a few months earlier. "Um... Sure."

"You're wondering why an older guy like me is in a place like this, huh?" he continued with a sly grin. "I'm not *that* old. Go on, guess how old I am!"

"I really don't know," she said, hoping to get away from what was becoming an increasingly awkward situation. "I should get back to my -"

"Forty-six," he said, cutting her off. "I probably seem like a total fossil to you. I'm the oldest guy in this club tonight by a good ten years, but that's just because most of the men my age are married off by their thirties. They get old and boring, and they don't like this kind of music. I love it, though. Give me a proper live band any day of the week. I used to be in a band, actually. We got pretty big for a while, we even went on a tour of Scandinavia once in my mate's camper van."

"That's great," she told him. "I should get going, though. Bye."

Turning away, she could only hope that he'd leave her alone now.

"We found more bones, you know," he added.

Stopping, she looked back at him.

"Yeah, I thought that'd get your interest," he continued, conspicuously looking her up and down. "We found more than one set of bones in that pit. Not at first, but later, when the crew turned up to make it safe. There was a partial male set down there as well, probably from around the same time that the Maitland woman died. Never publicized that fact, though. By that point the case was closed and everyone was busy with other stuff. Something that happened fifty years ago really didn't seem important. Sucks that things work that way in real life, but we don't have the resources to look through a bunch of cold cases."

He looked her up and down again, and this time his gaze lingered on her hips.

"Want to come and sit down with me, and we can talk about it?" he added lasciviously. "I bet I've got some more fun facts that you'd like to hear."

"Thanks, but I'm okay," she replied, turning and hurrying through the crowd, but also unable to stop thinking about everything he'd just told her.

"Great," Tommo said as he took his drink from her hand, "I was starting to think I might die of thirst here."

"I just found out the weirdest thing," she told him. "You know, I still think there are parts of what happened at Benson's that we never quite figured out."

***

"Stupid asshole!" Sasha hissed under her breath, bumping against one of the traffic lights before stopping and looking back toward the seafront. "Asshole!" she yelled at the top of her voice. "Do you hear me?"

She waited, but in truth she was pretty sure Derek hadn't heard her at all. After their argument in the club he'd stormed off in the opposite direction; she'd expected him to swing back round and try to make everything better, but now she realized that he really *had* gone somewhere else, which was technically what she'd told him to do even if secretly she'd been hoping to make up. Now, however, she felt her blood starting to boil as she realized that he didn't care enough to make her feel better.

"Asshole," she said again, sniffing back tears. "Am I not even worth fighting for?"

She looked along the High Street, and after a moment she paused as she saw that the lights were on at the coffee shop. Puzzled, she quickly remembered that deliveries were due on Thursdays, and she allowed herself a faint smile as she thought back to all those nights she used to spend chatting away to Josh. Although she absolutely didn't miss her job at the shoe shop, she realized now that in some small way she actually missed hanging out on the fire escape. She lingered for a moment longer, wondering whether she should start checking the pubs for any sign of Derek, but finally she told herself that she'd rather go and see Josh one more time.

"Screw Derek," she said, bumping against the window of the estate agent's office as she drunkenly made her way along the street. "Screw everyone. I'm worth better."

As she got closer to the shoe shop, she saw that the windows were boarded up, with pieces of plywood having been nailed all over the front. She stopped and stared at the boards, and she thought back to her dead-end job in that place, and she realized in a moment of surprise that she was actually feeling nostalgic. Wandering to the coffee shop, she looked inside and saw that all the lights were still on, although there was no sign of Josh. She reached out to open the door, only to find that it was locked.

"Hey!" she called out, banging gently on the glass. "Dude, are you in there?"

She waited, puzzled by the lack of a response.

"Hey!" she shouted a little louder, banging slightly harder. "Are you on the toilet or something? Wakey wakey!"

She waited again, and this time she spotted a hint of movement in the doorway that led to the storeroom. A shadow briefly moved across the wall before disappearing, and after a moment Sasha let out a sigh.

"Are you listening to something on headphones?" she sighed. "I'm right here, you idiot. Aren't you going to let me in?"

After a few seconds she stepped back, and she once again considered hunting for Derek in the pubs. She could think of half a dozen he might have gone to, but part of her wanted to really let him stew. She knew he'd be expecting her, and she wanted to show him that she didn't *have* to go running after him every time they had an argument. Finally, figuring that she could get a kick out of scaring Josh, she made her way past the coffee shop and round the corner, before heading into the supermarket parking lot. Approaching the back of the shops, she climbed over a small gate and then opened the door at the rear of the coffee shop, finding that it had been left open.

Once she was inside, she walked through the storeroom and through to the counter area. Looking around, she was surprised to find that there was no sign of Josh at all.

"Hey, are you here?" she called out, disappointed that she hadn't been able to sneak up on him. "Dude, it's me. Come on, I didn't come here for no reason, did I? Where are you hiding?"

She waited, unaware that Josh was now

standing right behind her, staring at the back of her head.

CHAPTER TWENTY-ONE

"OKAY," TOMMO SAID AS he followed Lisa away from the rear of Nelson's, heading out past the pitch-black library, "I get what you mean, but why does it matter? Old bones are just old bones. You can't change anything."

"Something's bugging me," she replied, walking ahead. "To be honest, I think it's been bugging me all this time and I just wasn't ready to admit it."

"Yeah, but... who actually cares?"

"Me!" she snapped, stopping and turning to him. "Listen, it's probably nothing, but I just want to be sure."

"And this isn't just an attempt to hang out with Josh again?"

"I'm not into Josh!" she protested.

"Say it all you want," he replied, "but no-one's going to believe you. You've always had a crush on him, and the sad thing is that you probably always will."

"That's not fair," she told him. "I just want to make sure that everything's sorted out. There was something wrong at the supermarket, Tommo, and I'm worried it might still be there. Josh and I were possessed by the ghosts of Dorothy Maitland and Walter Stryke, but their ghosts should have left when we found their bodies. That's how it works, isn't it? Once they're laid to rest, they should stop haunting the place."

"Haven't they?" he asked. "Serious question. What makes you think they're still haunting anywhere?"

"I just feel like..."

She paused, trying to make sense of the conflicting thoughts that were rushing through her mind. Every time she tried to understand what had happened, she came back to one lingering concern.

"That ghost was inside me," she continued. "It was controlling me, but I can't shake the strangest feeling that... it wasn't the ghost of Dorothy Maitland."

"Who was it, then?" he said, sounding increasingly exasperated. "I want to get back to the club in time for the band's last song."

"Then go," she replied, turning and hurrying

along the street. "I'm probably completely wrong, but I have to be sure!"

"Have fun chasing after Josh again," he said with a sigh, watching as she disappeared into the distance before turning and heading back toward the club. "Damn it. Why do I never get the girl?"

***

A few minutes later, as she reached the front of the coffee shop, Lisa stopped and looked through into the brightly-lit store. Behind her, a man was muttering to himself as he opened the door of his lorry and climbed up into his cab.

"Hey, you!" the man said. "Down there!"

Startled, Lisa turned to him.

"You don't know anything about this, do you?" he asked, nodding toward the shop.

"What do you mean?" she asked.

"I'm the delivery guy," he told her. "I come every Wednesday night and that lanky kid's always waiting for me with his attitude. He's not here tonight, though. I've even tried calling the shop's phone, I hear it ringing in there but he doesn't pick up."

"That's not like Josh," she replied. "He's very conscientious."

"The crazy part is," he continued, "I think someone *is* in there. I'm sure I spotted a shadow moving. Anyway, I've been hammering on the door for twenty minutes and he clearly isn't going to answer, and I've got ten more stops to make so I can't hang around any longer. His boss won't be happy in the morning, though, when he finds out they didn't get the delivery. If you ask me, not opening up for the delivery should be a firing offense. If you see that kid, tell him I'm not impressed!"

With that, he started the engine and drove away, leaving Lisa to look once again at the shop. She hurried to the door and pulled the handle, only to find that it was locked in place. Peering through the glass, she spotted the faintest hint of a shadow on the far wall, as if someone was moving around in the storeroom at the back.

"Josh!" she called out, banging on the door. "Hey, can you hear me? Josh!"

She banged again, but she could already tell that she wasn't going to have any luck. Deep down, she couldn't shake an instinctive worry that something must be wrong; as much as Josh hated his job, she knew that he'd always dutifully stuck around waiting for the delivery guy, so his absence now had to mean that something was wrong. And then, a moment later, she heard a faint and muffled cry coming from somewhere inside the shop, as if someone briefly tried to call out.

"Josh!" Lisa yelled, before making her way

along the High Street, figuring that she could try the coffee shop's back door. "Okay, there's nothing actually wrong," she continued, trying to calm her fears as she walked round the corner and headed toward the supermarket's parking lot. "You're just... checking, that's all. You're checking that everyone's fine, and then you'll be able to go home and watch Alex Mack repeats and chill out and -"

"Help!" a female voice shouted suddenly. "Somebody help me!"

Lisa froze for a moment, before hurrying toward the parking lot's entrance just in time to see Sasha racing away from the rear of the row of shops. A moment later a second figure appeared, chasing after her; Sasha tripped and fell, and by the time she got back to her feet Josh had already caught up to her again.

"Get away from me!" Sasha shouted, struggling violently as Josh wrapped his arms around her and tried to drag her back toward the coffee shop. "Leave me alone!"

"Stop!" Lisa shouted, running over to them. "Josh, what are you doing?"

"This is none of your business!" he sneered angrily, looking up at her. "You shouldn't even be here, you -"

Before he could finish, Sasha bit his wrist. Letting out a cry of pain, he fell back as Sasha stumbled to her feet and ran over to the rear of the supermarket, where she proceeded to frantically pull on the locked door.

"It's happening again," Lisa stammered. "I was right, it's -"

Before she could finish, she saw that another building had appeared in the same space as the supermarket. She stared with a growing sense of shock at the sight of the old church, which seemed to have returned as a kind of ghost, superimposed over the supermarket and rising up high into the night sky.

Suddenly Josh shoved her to the ground, before setting off after Sasha again. Landing hard on her side and immediately rolling over, Lisa took a moment to get her breath back before sitting up. She looked toward the supermarket and saw that although she could easily run in any other direction, Sasha seemed absolutely determined to get through the locked door. Josh had already caught up to her again, and Lisa watched with a growing sense of horror as she saw him picking up a large rock from the ground.

"What are you doing?" she whispered as Josh raised the rock up high, as if he was about to bring it crashing down against the back of Sasha's head. "Josh, no!"

"You're supposed to be mine!" Josh snarled as Sasha sobbed and pulled on the door. "If that can't happen in life, then it's going to have to happen in death instead."

With that, he slammed the stone down toward Sasha's head, only for Lisa to grab his arm at the last second and pull him back. The stone fell harmlessly to the ground, but Lisa quickly found that she could barely pull Josh back at all. Shocked by his strength, she finally managed to force him down onto the ground, even as he struggled furiously to break free.

"Help me!" Sasha wept, dropping to her knees now and clawing at the door as if she still expected to somehow break into the supermarket. "Somebody, please... you have to help me!"

"Let go of me!" Josh snapped at Lisa as she struggled to hold him down. "You're interfering with something that has nothing to do with you!"

"I think it's got plenty to do with me!" she hissed. "In fact -"

In that moment, Josh shoved her aside and immediately rushed over to Sasha again. Grabbing her arm, he began to pull her away from the door even as she tried to reach out yet again for the handle.

"You're coming back with me," he told her, "and you're never going to get away from me again. Do you understand? We're going to be together forever and there's nothing you can do about it!"

"Josh?" Lisa said.

"What?" he shouted, turning to her. "Didn't I

_"

Swinging her fist, Lisa punched him hard on the side of the face, knocking him out instantly and sending him crumpling to the ground.

"Wow!" Lisa gasped, shocked by her own strength even as she felt a rippling pain in her knuckles. Looking down, she was just about able to unclench her fist, although the pain remained and now she was shaking with fear. She turned to Sasha, who was now simply staring up at her. "Wow!" Lisa said again. "Just... wow!"

CHAPTER TWENTY-TWO

FOR A MOMENT, THE three of them simply sat in silence in the coffee shop, on a trio of chairs arranged in a circle. No-one knew what to say; Josh had a pack of ice pressed against one side of his head, while Sasha was staring ahead as she tried to come to terms with what had happened and Lisa was still testing her fist to make sure that nothing was broken.

"So," Sasha said finally, figuring that the silence had to end at some point, "that was... odd."

"I wasn't myself," Josh replied. "I swear, you have to believe me, I'd never do something like that."

"I know," Sasha said, although she sounded a little uncertain. "I think."

"It must have been Walter Stryke again,"

Josh continued. "You know, now I'm aware of it, I don't think it's really stopped since that night all those months ago. The possession, I mean. I think it's been lingering, and Sasha... when you showed up again tonight, that sort of brought it bubbling back up to the surface."

"I wasn't myself tonight, either," Sasha admitted. "I could feel something else inside me, some other presence."

"That's Dorothy Maitland," Josh told her. "It has to be."

"It's not Dorothy Maitland," Lisa said.

They turned to her.

"And it's not Walter Stryke," she added. "Think about it, Josh. We acted the same way when we were possessed before, and we assumed it must be Dorothy and Walter, but it wasn't. "

"Then who possessed us?"

Lisa hesitated, as if she still couldn't quite believe what she was about to say.

"It was the same ghosts that possessed Dorothy and Walter back in 1949. And I think I saw the ghost of the church. Can buildings even have ghosts? Anyway, I think something else was possessing Dorothy and Walter all those years ago."

"Come again?" Josh replied.

"They were possessed that night, just like we were possessed. My theory is that Walter chased Dorothy into the ruined church and they both fell into a crack created by the bomb. They died, and Walter's family was too embarrassed to admit the truth so they literally knocked the church down and had the supermarket built over the bodies so that the truth would never come out. Then Walter's twin brother pretended to be him for a little while, just long enough to let the department store fail, before leaving and never coming back. The great and the good of Crowford were probably all in on the cover-up, they thought they'd done a great job, but what they didn't realize was that Walter and Dorothy were just victims of something else that night."

She paused for a few seconds.

"If Oswald Stryke had just had more faith in his brother, and hadn't accepted he'd do something like that, the truth might have come out sooner."

"Okay," Josh said cautiously, "but if we believe that theory – and it's still quite a big ask – then what are we supposed to do now? Who's actually been possessing people here?"

"I keep thinking back to the hole in the ground," Lisa told him. "The one I went down. It ended under the supermarket, but it extended under the parking lot in a straight line. I didn't get to explore all of it, but I think if I had, it would have led me to one place."

"Where?" Josh asked.

Lisa stared at him for a moment, and then

she looked down at the floor of the coffee shop. Josh did the same, as did Sasha a few seconds later.

"Wait," Josh continued, "are you saying... do you think there's something underneath us right now?"

***

"This is the most rank place I've ever been in my life," Sasha said as the light flickered on, illuminating the damp and dirty basement area beneath the coffee shop. "Do we really have to be down here?"

"Look!" Lisa said, heading to the far wall and pointing at a crack in the concrete floor. "It runs under here..."

She began to follow the crack, ducking her head down so she could step beneath a low arch.

"All the way through to here," she continued.

"That's the shoe shop," Sasha explained, heading after her. "The cheap skanks didn't even bother to divide the basement when they were carving up the old department store. How sketchy is that?"

"This is the other end of the crack that we found in the supermarket," Lisa said, reaching down and using her fingers to crumble some of the concrete away. "It's not very solid, either." She thought for a moment, still desperately trying to draw all the disparate strands together. "During the Second World War, a bomb hit the church and turned it into nothing more than ruins," she reminded them, "but what if that didn't actually create the crack in the ground and the hole and all that stuff? What if it only reopened it?"

"So where did it originally come from?" Josh asked.

"There's something under here," Lisa said, looking up at him. "Something has been under here for a very long time. I'm not just talking about the fifty years since the war, I'm talking centuries before that, possibly even longer. Something has been buried under here, held down beneath the pressure of the ground, but the bomb created a weak point that allowed a tiny crack to get much bigger. Something under these shops has been trying to break out for years, and thanks to the bomb it was able to reach up and..."

Again she paused; her mind was racing and she felt as if she was on the verge of coming up with the answer.

"And take control of the people it found on the surface," she added finally. "Moving them around like puppets, controlling them, using them to replay what had happened over and over again."

"Why?" Sasha asked. "To remember good times?"

"Or as some kind of warning?" Josh suggested.

Lisa scratched at the crack's edges for a moment longer, and she was surprised to find that more chunks were coming away fairly easily.

"Or both," she said softly. "What if this thing is bigger than we realized?"

For a few seconds she thought of the chaos at Nelson's, of the drunks having arguments, of Detective Marshall's leering eye and aggressive come-ons, of Sasha screaming at her date, of all the violence and anger that she'd witnessed since she'd first been old enough to sneak into the locals pubs and clubs. She thought of her own father, who'd never needed alcohol to turn his fists on his family, and she thought of the way Crowford had become such a drab and miserable place even though news reports always claimed that the country was on the way up. She knew she couldn't blame all of that on whatever was emanating from the crack in the ground, but she supposed that there might be some mix of responsibility. She also knew that Crowford supposedly had a long and extensive network of tunnels running beneath its streets, and she found herself wondering whether some kind of negativity might even be using those tunnels to spread faster and further than it might otherwise manage.

All just theories, of course, but ones that she found interesting.

"We're going to dig," she whispered finally, before looking up at Josh and Sasha. "We're going to dig it up."

"Dig *what* up?" Josh asked.

"I don't know," she told him, "but there's something down here and we haven't managed to stop it yet. So we're going to dig, and I think the ground is already so badly damaged that we'll find it easier than it should be. I don't know how far down we'll have to go -"

She checked her watch.

"- but it's almost midnight now, so that gives us a few hours."

"What am I going to tell Betty and the others when they come to work in the morning and find a big hole in the basement?" Josh replied.

"You said it yourself, people barely come down here," Lisa said, getting to her feet. "You don't have to help, not if you don't want to. You can blame me in the morning, and you might be right, this might be a waste of time. There might not be anything down there, or we might never be able to get deep enough, but we have to try! Josh, do you *ever* want to feel that thing possessing you again and making you do those awful things? I know you're not that kind of person."

"No," he said after a moment, shaking his head, "I'm not. At least, I try not to be. And you're right, I hated that more than anything."

"Well, I'm in," Sasha added. "Any excuse to damage someone else's property is fine as far as I'm concerned."

"I know where to get some shovels," Josh said. "The garden center down the road has a load, they leave them out in their delivery yard. It's not stealing if we clean them and return them by sunrise, is it?"

CHAPTER TWENTY-THREE

1942...

THE CHURCH STOOD IN silence, dark and unattended.

Inside, neat rows of pews lined either side of the central aisle. Had anyone cared to inspect closely, they would have spotted the faintest crack running along the tiled floor, snaking beneath some of the pews.

In the distance, a whistling sound was getting louder, descending rapidly from above until finally a German bomb crashed through the church's roof, slamming into the ground and exploding instantly. A huge ball of fire burst through the space, blowing out the windows and destroying not only the roof but also parts of the walls.

***

1949...

"Dorothy, wait!" Walter shouted as he hurried out through the door at the back of Stryke Brothers. "Dorothy, you've got me all wrong! I was just proposing a little fun, that's all!"

He saw her in the distance, rushing out across the moonlit grass and heading toward the ruined church. For a moment he stopped, assuming that there was no point trying to catch her, but after a few seconds he set off again, determined to grab her and make her understand that he hadn't meant anything bad. Huffing and puffing, and desperately out of shape, his attempt to run was barely any faster than walking pace, but after a couple of minutes he'd reached the old crumbling doorway that led into what had once been the church. He stopped again, trying to get his breath back, before stepping through into the darkness.

"Dorothy," he continued, barely managing to get any words out, "you really don't need to hide from me. I just thought that you could show me a little gratitude, that's all. Honestly, I don't know what came over me."

Looking along the moonlit aisle, under a shattered roof that had been blown away several years earlier, he saw the remains of old pews scattered around. A huge gaping hole had opened up in the floor, cracking open the tiles and leaving a dark gap. Walter stepped closer to the edge and looked down, before glancing over his shoulder. He waited, listening to the silence, but he heard nothing.

"Dorothy, are you here?" he called out, before turning to hurry back outside, convinced that she'd given him the slip. "Dorothy, I just want a chance to explain. I feel like... I feel I wasn't quite being myself and -"

Before he could finish, he heard a scrambling sound, followed seconds later by a gasp. He looked around the moonlit ruins again, before stepping back to the hole in the ground and looking down. This time, he was just about able to make out something moving a little way inside the hole, and to his horror he realized that Dorothy was clinging to a large root poking out from the side.

"What are you doing down there?" he stammered. "Dorothy -"

"Help me!" she sobbed, already starting to lose her grip on the root. "I fell! Please, fetch somebody to help me!"

"There's no time for that," he said, as he started trying to climb down to rescue her. "Dorothy, you'll just have to trust me. What happened back there, it wasn't really me. Something just comes over me from time to time, I know that's no excuse but... Just take my hand, okay?" He reached down toward her. "Hurry!"

"Don't touch me!" she snapped.

"Dorothy, I understand why you're scared of me," he replied, "but I'm really just trying to help you. Once you're up and safe, you can call me all the names under the sun, you can tell everybody that I'm an awful man, but please... first, you have to let me get you to safety." He leaned a little further into the hole, straining to reach her. "Dorothy, please, you must -"

In that moment he lost his footing. Tumbling forward, he let out a brief cry as he plummeted into the hole, falling past Dorothy and disappearing into the darkness before a heavy thud rang out far below. Screaming, Dorothy almost fell as well, only just managing to cling to the root.

"Mr. Stryke?" she shouted. "Are you alright? Can you hear me?"

She looked down, but she couldn't even see the bottom of the hole. Realizing that she needed to haul herself to safety, she looked up again and tried to work out a route. She spotted several other roots sticking out from the mud, and after a moment she reached up for one of them; once she was sure that her grip was solid, she began to pull. For a few seconds she felt as if she might actually manage, but seconds later the root broke and she fell. Another root, sticking out in the moonlight, caught the side of her throat with its sharp tip, ripping the flesh away and letting blood burst from her body.

Landing in a cradle of other roots, Dorothy reached up and grasped her throat, but she was already too late. Hot blood was gushing from her body, and as she let out a few dying groans she looked up and saw the starry sky above as her blood dribbled down and fell deeper into the hole in the ground.

***

The following morning, Eric Grace stood at the edge of the pit and stared down at Dorothy's corpse. One of his workers was in the process of climbing up, and the man finally hauled himself over the edge.

"It's as you feared, Sir," Arnold explained. "Mr. Stryke's body is down at the very bottom. It's going to be difficult to bring him up."

"This church has stood ruined for years," Eric muttered, looking around at the scene of devastation. "It's on my land so it's my choice what to do with it. I'm starting to think that I've spent too long listening to all the weak-willed fools who think the place should be rebuilt. It's not as if any of them are offering to put their money in. Do you know what I hate in this town more than anything? I hate people who demand that things are done, and demand that other people put their hands in their pockets to pay for it!"

He turned and looked over at his twenty-nine-year-old daughter Angela, who was hanging back near the ruined doorway.

"Come closer, girl," he said, gesturing for her to join him. "You need to see this."

"Father -"

"You're not like your sister," he continued. "She has a certain weakness in her mind, but you're the strong one."

Angela hesitated for a moment, before making her way over. As soon as she spotted Dorothy's body, she let out a shocked cry and turned away.

"Yes," Eric muttered, "I agree."

He paused for a moment, lost in thought, before turning to Arnold.

"The time has come to make a decision," he sneered. "The way I see it, we have two options. The first option is that we let everyone know what has happened here. Walter Stryke's name will be dragged through the mud, the department store he built up will probably face ruin, and the family of Dorothy Maitland will know the sorry details of her final moments. The result will be horrific for the entire town." He paused again. "The other option is that we use this as an opportunity. I'll have the church knocked down and this hole in the ground covered over, with the bodies left down there to rot. Then I'll find someone to take the place off my hands and put a nice new building on top, and the truth will be covered forever."

"What about the bodies?" Arnold asked. "It doesn't seem right to leave them there, somehow."

"This was a church, was it not?" Eric replied. "Seems to me, that makes this hallowed ground." He turned to his daughter. "Of course, the decision doesn't have to be up to me. Angela, it's time for you to start making some hard choices in life. After all, I shan't be around forever and one day you'll have to take charge. Your sister's too simple-minded to do it, so the burden will fall onto your shoulders." Reaching out and taking her by the hand, he forced her to turn again and look back down into the hole.

"Father," she said, with tears in her eyes, "I -"

"What will it be?" he asked. "This is a moment that will change your character forever, my dear. Will you be weak and allow the town to suffer as a result? Or will you be strong and do the right thing, even if that means risking unpopularity?"

"I..."

For a few seconds, she had no idea what to say. Finally, however, she felt a strange hardening of her heart, and the tears disappeared from her eyes even as she kept her gaze fixed on the sight of Dorothy's corpse.

"Cover it over," she said after a moment. "All of it. Cover it over, and then call Walter Stryke's brother and explain what has happened. In fact, I think I have an idea of how we can wrap this whole mess up rather neatly."

CHAPTER TWENTY-FOUR

1998...

LETTING OUT A GROAN, Lisa stopped for a moment as a painful stitch rippled up through one side of her belly. She and the others had been digging or a couple of hours now, and they'd made decent progress, but none of them could be sure that their work was going to yield anything at all.

"Is anyone else exhausted?" Josh asked, as he too took a break. "I didn't know I was so unfit. This is like hard labor!"

"Wimps!" Sasha muttered, as she used her right foot to push the shovel's tip deeper into the muddy ground beneath the layer of crumbling concrete. "I expected better from both of you. You're not giving up, are you?"

"How far are we going to dig?" Josh continued, turning to Lisa. "All the way to China?"

"We need to keep going for a little while longer," she told him, still trying to get her breath back. "The crack starts here, so it's reasonable to assume that this is where something's buried. If I'm wrong, I'm wrong, and I'll take the blame for that. I already told you that you don't have to help, not if you don't want to."

"Are you two just going to stand around talking?" Sasha asked, as she continued to dig.

"If I'm wrong," Lisa said to Josh, "then that leaves us all the way back at square one."

"It's not our fight," he pointed out. "At least, it doesn't have to be. Once we're out of Crowford, we can forget about it all. Let it be someone else's problem."

"I know that's a possibility," Lisa admitted, "but -"

"But nothing," he said firmly. "Why should we go to all this trouble when no-one else has ever bothered?"

"Is that you talking," she replied, "or is something else influencing your thoughts?"

"It's me," he told her, before pausing again. "I think."

"That's exactly my point," she told him. "Until we've stopped this, whatever it turns out to be, how can any of us be absolutely sure that we're not still being influenced? I don't know about you, but I'd really like to know for certain that my thoughts are my own."

"Fine," Josh said, "but -"

Suddenly they both heard a thudding sound, and they turned just as Sasha stopped digging. Her shovel was still in the ground, and after a moment she turned to them.

"I hit something," she said, with a hint of shock in her voice. "I think... I think it's wooden."

"Let me see," Lisa replied, stepping over and dropping to her knees, using her hands now to pull away more mud. "You're right, there's definitely something here," she continued excitedly, brushing away yet more dirt to reveal what appeared to be some kind of flat wooden surface. "What is it?"

"Hang on," Josh said, as he and Sasha knelt on either side of her and got to work, "I think..."

He fell silent as he dug more dirt away, and then he pulled back.

"It's a coffin," he added.

"Are you sure?" Sasha asked.

"Well, it's a long rectangular box buried in the ground," he replied, turning to her, "so what else could it be?"

"You're right," Lisa said, clambering around to the other side as the shape of the coffin began to emerge from the soil. "It's definitely a coffin. It must have been down here for centuries!"

"Okay, this is getting spooky again," Sasha pointed out. "I know I was totally up for that before, but now I'm starting to wonder whether we're getting too involved in something we don't understand. I almost died when I got pushed down those stairs, remember? This could be dangerous."

"She's right," Josh said after a moment, watching as Lisa examined the coffin's lid. "We should probably go and call someone who knows about this sort of thing. I don't quite know who that would be, but the police might be the best start."

"Yeah," Lisa said, fiddling with the sides of the lid, "because they did such a great job last time."

"But -"

"If you want, go and find Detective Marshall. Right about now he's probably puking his guts up behind Nelson's."

"Seriously?" Josh replied, raising both eyebrows. "I didn't think old dudes liked that sort of music."

"Got it!" Lisa said suddenly, as she managed to lift part of the coffin's lid. "It's not even nailed in place. Either that, or the wood's so rotten that the nails are no longer holding it. Can you guys try lifting different parts? If we're lucky, we should be able to get this whole thing open."

"And see the dead body inside?" Josh said.

"Is that definitely what we're wanting to do here?"

"Hell, yes," Sasha replied with a smile as she crawled to the other end of the lid and began to lift. "After everything that's been happening, I damn well want to see what's behind it all. Or who."

"Fine," Josh said as he set to work helping with the lid. "You know, I remember when I got my job at the coffee shop, people told me I'd go insane from the boredom. Frankly, right now a spell of boredom doesn't sound too bad at all. I'd quite like to be bored out of my mind instead of digging up corpses and trying to stop evil ghosts and -"

Suddenly the lid came loose, and all three of them fell back against the sides of the hole they'd been digging. Lisa immediately moved the lid out of the way, and then they all looked down into the coffin and saw a skeletal figure.

"Okay," Josh said cautiously, "so... who is this guy? Or girl?"

"Look," Lisa replied, pointing at a pair of skeletal hands resting on the chest. "Notice anything? There are hands there, and also down there."

"This person had four arms?" Josh suggested skeptically.

Reaching into the coffin, Lisa very carefully tried to move the skull aside, revealing a second skull beneath.

"There are two bodies in here," she said

after a few seconds. "There are two *complete* sets of bones, one on top of the other. And the one on the bottom seems to be holding the other one, almost like an embrace."

"So were they husband and wife?" Sasha asked. "You know, I think I've heard about stuff like that before. Back in the old days, sometimes married couples who died together were buried in the same coffin. I kind of assumed they weren't stuffed together like sardines in a tin, but I guess this would have been the cheaper way to do it all."

"Maybe," Lisa whispered, peering more closely at the discolored bones.

"It's kind of romantic in a way," Josh observed.

Sasha turned to him with a scowl.

"I mean it!" he protested. "Think about it for a moment. These two were so in love that they couldn't bear to be parted, not even in death. So they were buried like this, one with their arms around the other, left alone for all eternity to just be together. You guys can call me sentimental if you like, but I don't care. All I've ever wanted in my life is to find someone I truly love, and who feels the same way about me in return. I consider that to be the ultimate ideal, the pinnacle of human life, and I for one envy these two for finding that kind of love."

"Dude, stop," Sasha said, rolling her eyes,

"you're making me want to gag."

"Don't you want that kind of love?" he asked, sounding a little disappointed.

"Love's overrated," she told him. "It's this thing that people strive for, it's a way of closing off their connections to the rest of the world. If you ask me, life's about living every day to the max, and love stops you doing that. Love's a prison inside a gilded cage, and nothing you say can ever persuade me otherwise. I can't imagine ever feeling so strongly for someone that I'd actually want my dead ass buried with them. Call me crazy if you want, but as far as I'm concerned that's way too much love."

"I think it's romantic," Josh replied.

"Well," Sasha said, "I think it's stupid."

"It's also irrelevant," Lisa added, causing them both to turn to her as she pointed at the hands wrapped around the top body's chest. "Look here. And here. Do you see the way the bottom body is holding the other one?"

"It's a hug," Josh said. "Or an embrace."

"No, it's not," Lisa continued. "It's totally unnatural for an embrace." She stared for a moment longer before turning to him. "The bottom body wasn't hugging the other one. It was holding it down. I think it was trying to stop it escaping."

CHAPTER TWENTY-FIVE

"I HEARD ABOUT SOMETHING like this once before," Josh said cautiously, as they stared down at the intertwined skeletons. "There were rumors that some bodies were found like this when the car park behind the library was built. Just rumors, though."

"Crowford certainly seems to be a place for weird shit," Sasha suggested, wrinkling her nose slightly. "But you're right, Lisa. In this particular case, the dead guy's starting to seem a little... clingy. I think this is like the exact opposite of the other case. Like two sides of the same coin, though."

"We don't know that it's a guy," Lisa pointed out.

"Sure," she replied, "but... I mean, what are the odds?"

"There's something on the lid," Josh said, stepping over to the upturned lid and moving it so that he could read the text better. "Something's been written on the inside."

"Let me see," Lisa added, as she and Sasha headed over to join him.

"It's kind of hard to make out," he continued, squinting a little. "There's something about... some names. I can't read them properly, though."

"It's too old and too rotten," Lisa remarked.

"I think there's something there with a number," Josh said, reaching out and pointing at one section of the lid. "Is that a number six, or maybe an eight?"

"Possibly." Leaning closer, Lisa saw various semi-legible letters, but she felt her frustration growing as she realized that actually reading the text was going to be almost impossible. "So the bit at the top might be names," she suggested. "It's more centered and it seems to be separate from the rest of the text."

"Like on a gravestone?" Josh asked.

"Definitely like a gravestone," she muttered, before spotting a few letters that she could actually make out. "That name starts with an M," she added, reaching out and touching the rotten wood. "Then there's -"

***

December 1842...

Exactly one hundred and fifty-six years earlier, an icy wind blew through Crowford, whistling through the narrow gaps of houses lining either side of pitch-black Down Street.

A lone figure shuffled through the snow, with her shawl pulled tight in a desperate attempt to retain at least a small amount of warmth. She saw lights ahead and heard laughter, drifting out from *The Pelican*, but she didn't dare to enter any of the town's public houses. Indeed, she quickened her pace as she passed this particular building, for she knew that this was one of the many parts of town frequented by a certain gentleman she was keen to avoid.

"Evening, Hannah," a voice called out, as an elderly woman leaned out from the window of a house on the corner. "Not the kind of night you want to be out and about."

"I have to fetch some items for my uncle," Hannah replied, forcing a smile. "He's working very late and he needs ink."

"Should've planned ahead a little, shouldn't he?" the woman muttered. "What's he got to write about that's so important, anyway?"

"I really don't know" Hannah said as she made her way past, "but he insists that it's most urgent. I don't mind going, anyway. In fact, I rather enjoy running errands for him. He's a very important man!"

She heard the woman shouting a reply, but in truth Hannah had no desire to keep talking. She was passing another pub now, and she was briefly bathed in the lights of *The Goose and Magnet* before hurrying on. Ahead she saw the lights of *The Draper*, the northernmost such place on Down Street, and she told herself that soon she'd be able to breathe a little easier. She passed those lights too, and now she could see the door of Mr. Randall up ahead, and she allowed herself to hope that she might yet proceed unmolested.

"Ms. Marley?" a voice said suddenly, creaking and groaning in the cold night air. "Is that you?"

Stopping, she felt a rush of fear in her chest. Having waited until nightfall, despite her father's protestations, Hannah had been hopeful that she might avoid Jacob Stadwyck; the elderly man's voice cut through her now, however, and as she slowly turned and looked back toward the doorway of *The Draper* she saw his unmistakable silhouette in front of the dim firelight flickering inside the building. Her first thought was to turn and run, or to mumble an excuse, but a moment later Stadwyck stepped out onto the street, leaning heavily on his cane as he approached.

"I thought I recognize those dainty steps," he purred, "and that hurried breath. What brings such a perfect young creature out into these violent streets, especially at so late an hour?"

"I'm just on an errand," she replied, struggling to resist the urge to scream.

"You shouldn't be sent on errands at this time," he continued, making his way closer until he was just a couple of feet away. "Your father should know better. If you were my daughter, or my wife, or anything to do with me... I would rather die than subject you to such an ordeal."

"I should be going, Mr. Stadwyck," she said firmly. "My father -"

"Your father does not appreciate you," he replied, before she could get another word out. "That much is painfully clear. You're such a beautiful young lady, and -"

Suddenly he broke into a terrible coughing fit. Startled, Hannah watched as the old man stumbled back against the wall; she loathed Jacob Stadwyck with every fiber of her being, but after a moment she stepped forward and tried to help him, holding him up even as his withered body seemed set to slump down against the filthy pavement.

"You're too kind!" he gasped. "It's nothing, I'm quite alright!"

"Perhaps you shouldn't be out so late," she suggested.

"Then when would I get to see your pretty face?" he stammered, wiping spittle from his lips. "You so rarely make an appearance, Ms. Marley. Would it surprise you to learn that I often loiter here late at night, hoping to catch you on one of your father's ill-timed errands?"

"There's really no need for that, Mr. Stadwyck," she replied.

"I would do anything to see you more regularly," he told her. "You are even prettier than the Bond girl."

"That's kind of you to say so," she murmured, although she knew Stadwyck's words were mere flattery. He had a reputation for becoming obsessed with young ladies around the town, showering them with gifts and affection in a deluded attempt to win their hand in marriage. Almost every year a different girl became the object of his amorous lust, and Hannah had been hoping for a while that he would soon turn his attention elsewhere. "You should go back inside, Mr. Stadwyck," she continued. "It's not good for you to be out here in the cold."

"I'm fine," he replied. "I -"

He immediately broke into another coughing fit. Hannah patted him hard on the back, and after a few seconds she saw that a fine smattering of blood had sprayed from his mouth, leaving flecks all over his hands. In that instant she realized that the old man was clearly sick, and that most likely he would soon succumb to whatever malady was causing him to cough so violently.

"I shall be quite alright!" he gasped breathlessly, before reaching out and gripping Hannah hard on the arm. "At least... I shall be if I have you by my side. Won't you consider becoming my housekeeper, Ms. Marley? I would pay you handsomely and you could live in the part of my house that used to be reserved for servants. I assure you, you would be looked after properly, and your duties..."

He paused, before reaching over and squeezing her chest.

"Your duties would be light," he continued, "and -"

"Get off me!" she snapped angrily, slapping the side of his face as she pulled back. "Mr. Stadwyck, you mustn't go around touching people like that! Have you completely taken leave of your senses?"

"I like the fact that you fight back," he snarled. "I like it when you wriggle."

"I shall tell my father about your behavior," she continued, stepping back a little further. "How do you think he'll react, Mr. Stadwyck? What do you think people all across the town will say?"

"You'll be mine eventually," he replied firmly. "You don't know it yet, but one day you'll be in my arms, and I shall hold you so very tenderly as I caress your body."

"Never!" she hissed, before turning and hurrying away along the darkened street. "You should be utterly ashamed of yourself!"

"I *know* you'll be mine," he muttered as he watched her disappear around the corner. "Wriggle as much as you want, my dear, but eventually you will be in my arms."

CHAPTER TWENTY-SIX

ONE MONTH LATER, EDWARD Marley stood in the undertaker's backroom and stared down at his daughter's body in the coffin. With tears in his eyes, Edward watched Hannah's face, hoping for even the faintest hint of life, for the slightest chance that the doctor might have been wrong. Deep down, however, he knew that there had been no mistake, and that his only child had now been snatched away.

"Mr. Marley," a voice said, drifting into the room from nearby, "if you need more -"

"I'm done, thank you," Edward replied, wiping tears from his cheek as he turned and headed toward the door. "I just wanted to see her one more time, that's all. You can seal the coffin."

"Of course," Mr. Gresham said, briefly doffing his hat as Edward hurried away. "I shall do so immediately."

Stepping into the room, the undertaker made his way around the coffin before stopping to look down at Hannah's dead, waxy face. A moment later he heard footsteps, and he glanced up just in time to see the young boy Percy following him into the room.

"Please, Sir," Percy said cautiously, "I saw Mr. Marley leaving. Does that mean we're to prepare the lady for burial?"

"That would be the usual procedure," Mr. Gresham muttered, "but in this instance there is to be a slight... change to how we do things. You must remember, boy, that the work of an undertaker is hard yet undervalued. Why, I barely make enough money to scrape by. This poor young woman died quite suddenly, and Doctor Hardacre wasn't quite able to determine the cause. Apparently she had been sickening for a number of days before she had to be rushed to see the doctor, and she died within hours."

"She looks young," Percy said, stopping on the other side of the coffin and looking down at Hannah's corpse. "About my age, in fact. I don't like thinking what can happen to a person, one moment they seem fit and healthy, then the next they're in one of our coffins. Meanwhile poor Mr. Marley had to scrape together the money to give his daughter a proper burial, and now she's going to rot down there in the ground all alone."

"You're a good boy," Mr. Gresham replied. "Honest. Reliable. Decent."

He paused for a moment, before fishing about in his pocket and pulling out some coins.

"Go down to the seafront and see what the fisherman are selling this morning," he said, handing the coins to Percy. "I'll be hungry soon and some cockles or whelks would go down nicely. And pick something up for yourself, too."

"Are you sure?"

"Go," the undertaken continued, taking him by the arm and leading him to the door. "Get me something I'm liable to enjoy, won't you?" He pushed the boy out of the room and into the yard. "Take your time, too. There's no need to hurry. I can handle everything here."

He waited as Percy walked away, and then he shut the door and slid the bolt across. Pausing for a moment, he stared into space as he felt a flicker of dread running through his body, and then he turned once more to look at Hannah's body in the coffin. Reaching into his pocket, he took out a bundle of money and weight it in his hand; tears were filling his eyes, although he quickly sniffed them away as he put the money back into his pocket.

"Lord," he murmured, "forgive me for what I'm about to do. I'm a poor man and I need the money, and I'm not hurting anyone, not really. I'm not doing anything worse than anyone else. If anyone's to blame for this awful mess, it's Doctor Hardacre. I'm just... doing what seems best." He made the sign of the cross against his chest. "No-one's going to know the awful truth, anyway," he added. "No-one except the worms."

***

"That was a beautiful service," Sarah Timms said, stopping next to Edward as the small crowd began to filter away from the grave. "Hannah would have been proud."

"It's not much of a stone, is it?" Edward replied, his eyes filled with tears as he looked down at the modest marker he'd been able to afford. "She was my whole life, especially after Emily died. She was everything to me, and I still couldn't keep her safe."

"Do you still not know exactly what afflicted her?" Sarah asked.

A cold wind blew across the modest yard. For those who couldn't afford to have their loved ones buried in the churchyard, this small patch of land in the center of the town was something of a compromise. A small fee secured a spot just beyond the grounds of the nearby church, although rumors had been spreading that this particular space might soon be sold off to the highest bidder.

"Doctor Hardacre said that it was probably scarlet fever," Edward explained, "although he couldn't quite understand why no-one else around her caught it. Just a strange version, he suggested, and he thinks we should all be thankful that Hannah managed to avoid getting the rest of us sick. That'd be just typical of her, wouldn't it? Even in her hour of need, she was thinking of others. It was so quick, though. She fell ill, Doctor Hardacre visited her and within a matter of hours..."

His voice trailed off.

"Would you like to come and eat supper with us tonight?" Sarah asked, placing a hand on the side of his arm. "I know you don't have anyone now, Edward, not after Emily dying and now Hannah. We have a place at our table, and I know Henry would very much like to offer you our hospitality."

"You don't have to take pity on me," he replied.

"It's not pity, it's love," she told him. "You're my cousin, remember? We're family and we have to stick together." Linking her arm around him, she began to lead him away from the grave. "We'll come back in a few days and leave some flowers for poor Hannah. We can tend to her grave, Edward, and show her that we haven't forgotten her. I think she'd like that."

"I don't know what I'll live for now," he

replied, following her toward the gate before stopping as he saw another fresh grave. "Jacob Stadwyck," he read aloud. "That old miser? I hadn't heard that he was dead too."

"I think someone mentioned it," Sarah told him. "I don't recall the details, but he certainly won't be missed very much around Crowford. As far as I could tell, he spent most of his time in the various public houses on Down Street, drinking far too much and generally being unpleasant to everyone who had the misfortune to engage him in conversation. I know I shouldn't speak ill of the dead, but men like Jacob Stadwyck have always given me the shivers. No wonder he was never able to find himself a wife."

"He tried to court Hannah for a while," Edward replied as they turned and made their way down the steps that led out of the cemetery. "Then again, I hear he tried to court every young woman that caught his eye. No wonder people used to give him a wide berth in the pubs."

Their voices continued in the distance, eventually drifting away to nothing; the cemetery was left in silence, with the gathered crowd having long since dispersed. Hannah Marley's grave stood in peace, although no-one except the undertaker Charles Gresham knew that the coffin six feet beneath the surface was in fact filled with nothing more than some bags of sand. Nearby, the grave of

Jacob Stadwyck also seemed peaceful; again, however, only Charles Gresham knew the truth about the awful contract that had been struck on a dark and rainy night several weeks earlier.

***

As her eyes flickered open in the darkness, Hannah felt herself emerging from a deep and dreamless sleep. She vaguely remembered that Doctor Hardacre had paid her a visit while she was sick, and that he'd promised to give her something that would help her get some rest. He'd made her eat something, and as she'd slipped away she'd heard him whispering a prayer under his breath, begging for forgiveness from the Lord.

"What?" she whispered now, as she realized that she could feel arms wrapped around her body from below, and that she was resting on a most uncomfortable object. "Where -"

"Hush!" Jacob Stadwyck's voice groaned, as his bony hand reached up and clamped its fingers across her mouth. "There's no need to panic. You're where you belong. With me. Forever."

She tried to pull free, only to find that she was in a narrow and very confined space. Indeed, the more she struggled, the more she realized that the very air itself seemed thin and cold.

"I'm dying, young lady," Jacob whispered

directly into her ear, "but I refuse to take my final breaths alone. And since you so steadfastly failed to spend time with me before, I took steps to make sure that you're with me for my last moments." As she began to struggle more frantically, he tightened his grip and pressed his hand down more firmly against her mouth. "That's good," he purred softly. "I like it when you wriggle. And now we shall be together forever."

CHAPTER TWENTY-SEVEN

1998...

"NO!" LISA GASPED, PULLING back from the overturned coffin lid as her mind echoed with the furious sound of Hannah Marley struggling all those years ago.

"What is it?" Josh asked. "What's wrong?"

"She was buried alive," she stammered, staring in horror at the two skeletons. "This was a cemetery."

"Huh?" Josh replied. "How could it be a cemetery?"

"It must have been attached to the church that got bombed," she told him.

"They wouldn't build shops over a cemetery," he said firmly, before a hint of doubt entered his voice. "Would they?"

"Anything's possible when money's involved," Lisa pointed out, "and the ground might have shifted a little, especially with a bomb having gone off." She looked at the skeletons for a moment longer as a tear ran down her cheek. "I saw it all," she continued, "in a flash. A guy named Jacob Stadwyck had them buried alive together so that he could be with her for the rest of time. She struggled, but there would have been no way for them to be saved. He held her down here and they died in the coffin."

"That's... horrific," Sasha said as a shiver passed through her body. "What kind of maniac would do something like that?"

"Someone who can't take no for an answer," Lisa suggested. "And they've been down here ever since, except the bomb disturbed them and maybe allowed their ghosts to break out from the grave. They must have been reliving things over and over ever since, whenever they got a chance to possess two living people. Even in death, Stadwyck never stopped pursuing her, and she always had to run."

"So let's get her out of here," Sasha said, reaching into the coffin and grabbing the top set of bones, starting to pull them out. "That poor bitch shouldn't have to spend a moment longer down here with some creepy dude who couldn't get laid properly."

"Be careful with those," Lisa said, trying to stop her. "Hey, don't -"

Before she could finish, Sasha slipped and partially fell into the coffin. As she tried to steady herself, Sasha's right foot fell hard into the grave and smashed straight through the skull of Hannah Marley, turning it into little more than dust.

"Whoops," Sasha said, wincing slightly. "My bad."

"Let's try to show some respect," Lisa suggested.

"Yeah, totally," Sasha continued, pulling her foot free and – in the process – breaking a little more of the skull. "Sorry."

"So how do we end this?" Josh asked. "How do we make sure they never possess anyone else ever again? Because I've got to tell you guys, I really didn't enjoy having this asshole controlling me. I was almost able to push him out, but not quite. Then again, that might have been because I thought his name was Walter Stryke. I don't know, it might be easier now that I know his real name was... Jeremiah? Jebediah?"

"Jacob," Lisa reminded him. "Jacob Stadwyck."

"That's the dude," he continued, adjusting his collar a little as if he felt increasingly uncomfortable. Looking down at the one intact skull still in the coffin, he felt a shudder run through his bones. "Do you think he put all those horrible thoughts in my head, or do you think he just... drew out things that were already in there? It feels a little too easy for me to blame *all* my actions on him. I mean, I chased both of you across the car park, and I'm not sure what would have happened if I hadn't been stopped."

"Maybe that kind of primitive aggression's in all of us," Lisa suggested, "and it just takes a little nudge for it to come out."

"I hope not," Josh said, shuddering again. "The worst part is, I think you might be right."

"We're in over our heads," Lisa continued after a moment. "This isn't some kind of Kirrin Island or Camp Jellyjam adventure that we can solve with pluck and courage. This is something really old and really powerful, and I don't know about you guys but I'd like to bring someone in who actually know what they're doing. Why don't we go upstairs and call... someone?"

"The police?" Josh replied.

"That might be a good place to start," she replied. "We're just going to have to find some way to get them to believe us."

***

"Officer, you're not listening to me," Josh said with a sigh as he stood in the storeroom, using the coffee shop's phone. "The ghost isn't in front of me right now, and there's no ectoplasm."

"Right," the guy on the other end of the line said, sounding distinctly amused by the whole story, "and just let me get this part straight." He took a moment to clear his throat. "This isn't the number to call when you've got a ghost problem. This is for the police, we only deal with bad guys who are actually alive. Do you know who to call when you've got a ghost? Huh, kid? Do you know? Come on, tell me. Who you gonna call?"

"This is infuriating," Josh said through gritted teeth.

"Give it to me," Lisa muttered, grabbing the phone from him. "Officer, my name is Lisa Winter and I can vouch for everything my friend just told you."

"Oh, you can?" the man on the phone said. "Well, why didn't you let me know sooner? I'll just call every available detective and tell them to get down to Al's in Crowford because some undead creep has been dug up in the basement. Does that kind of sum up the situation?"

"You're an idiot," Lisa told him.

"Let me try," Sasha sighed, taking the phone from her. "Dude, list up for a moment, okay? You don't know everything so just shut your face and let me try to educate you. We've dug up two corpses and they might be dead, but they're sure as hell not shy. They've been infecting people, or possessing them, or whatever you want to call it. Now, I'm not expecting a dunce like you to wrap your head around that information, but that's fine, we just need you to patch us through to whoever handles stuff like this. We can't be the first people from Crowford to call up complaining about a ghost, so you *must* have someone you can send."

She paused, with the phone still against her ear.

"Hello?" she added, pulling the phone away and looking at the receiver. "That bastard hung up on me!"

"I wonder why," Lisa said under her breath.

"The police can't hang up on you," Sasha hissed, already redialing the number of Crowford's police station. "There has to be, like, a law against that. They have to at least send someone out to take a look at this mess we're in. When I get back through to that guy, I'm going to let him know exactly what I think of him. This is an actual serious police matter we're involved in and I won't be fobbed off!" She paused as a voice answered the phone. "Yes, hello," she continued, "I was speaking to someone just now and he put the phone down on me. You'd really better not make the same mistake."

"This is hopeless," Josh said quietly to Lisa as Sasha continued to rant to whoever had the misfortune of being on the other end of the line. "I don't know what we're supposed to do."

"I'm going to take another look down there," she replied, heading to the door that led down into the shop's basement. "There has to be some kind of clue."

"Do you want company?" he asked.

"I think I just need some space," she explained. "I need to think straight, without any distractions. I feel like we're still missing something."

"Join the club," Josh muttered, watching as she disappeared from view before turning to Sasha, who was becoming more and more heated and animated as she began to berate the officer on the phone. "Sasha," he continued, "I don't think you're helping. Why don't you let me try again? I might be a little more... diplomatic."

"Of course I haven't been smoking anything I shouldn't have!" Sasha hissed angrily. "How dare you accuse me of that? I'm an honest, law-abiding citizen." She turned and winked at Josh. "I'm going to explain what's happened again nice and slowly, so that even an idiot like you should be able to understand, and then you're going to send a police car down so that one of your colleagues can take a look at the situation. Do we understand each other?"

She waited, before looking at the receiver.

"Again?" she snapped furiously, before starting to dial again. "Okay, third time lucky. And this time, I'd better get put through to someone who has at least half a brain!"

CHAPTER TWENTY-EIGHT

"JACOB STADWYCK," LISA WHISPERED, kneeling next to the coffin and leaning down to look at the dead man's bones. "You know, Jacob, that's such a thing as being too clingy."

Reaching down, she moved some of Hannah's bones aside so that she could get a better look at Jacob's skeleton. To her surprise, she saw that there was still some meat on his bones; not a lot, of course, but a few scraps still clung to his face and ribs, even extending down his arms. His jaw was hanging open, as if he'd died screaming, and Lisa couldn't help but wonder whether – at the last moment – he'd regretted burying himself alive with Hannah. Was any love worth such a gruesome end?

Upstairs, Sasha had resorted to yelling at the police officer who'd answered her latest call.

"What's it going to take for you to be at peace, huh?" Lisa continued, reaching down and brushing some dirt from next to Jacob's skull. "Did you really love Hannah, or was she just the latest in a long line of girls you became infatuated with? I got a glimpse of what happened, and I can't shake the feeling that you just liked younger ladies. How old was Hannah, anyway? She was too young for you, that's for sure. I don't think you even understood love. You just lusted after every poor soul who crossed your path."

She looked down at his skeletal hands, which were still holding Hannah tight. When she tried to pull his hands aside, she found that they were locked in place; she had to really pull hard before she was able to get them to move at all, but finally she was able to slowly lift Hannah's bones up from the coffin.

"She's spent long enough down here with you," she murmured. "It's time for her to get her own grave."

"Listen to me, you asshole!" Sasha was shouting upstairs. "You're clearly too dumb to understand, so let me explain it in a way that even a child would understand!"

"That's never going to bring results," Lisa said as she set Hannah's bones down gently on the floor. "We might as well -"

Suddenly she heard a scraping sound.

Turning, she looked down at Jacob's rotten bones, worried that they might somehow have moved; she stared for a moment, but she saw no hint of a disturbance and after a few seconds she told herself that she was simply letting her paranoid mind run amok.

"Maybe burying you separately will be enough," she suggested, as she picked out a few more of Hannah's bones. "You realize this has to end, Jacob, don't you? I suppose you should get credit for perseverance, but seriously, at some point you have to accept that enough's enough." She turned away from him and began to arrange Hannah's bones so that she could carry them upstairs. "As for you, Hannah," she continued, "we're going to get you away from this asshole. Now that it's all over, we'll get you a grave all of your own so that -"

Before she could finish, she heard the same scraping sound as before, except that this time it sounded a little louder and closer.

And higher.

She froze for a moment, telling herself that everything was fine, and then she began to turn. As she did so, however, a skeletal hand grabbed her shoulder from behind and a second, more rotten hand clamped tight over her mouth.

***

"Do I have to go down there myself?" Sasha snapped, angrily slamming the phone's receiver down. "Is that what it's going to take? Because I'll do it, Josh, I swear to God! And if that's what has to happen, they're going to regret the day they ignored my call!"

"Let's just calm down," he replied, glancing at the door to the basement but seeing that there was still no sign of Lisa. "I don't think antagonizing the police is really going to get us very far. If they're not going to help, then I figure we need to document everything and find someone else who'll listen."

He paused, before heading to the door and looking down the staircase. Opening his mouth, he was about to call out to Lisa when he heard a bumping sound; supposing that she was busy, and not wanting to crowd her, he turned to Sasha again.

"What about a priest?" he asked.

"What priest?"

"There are churches in Crowford," he continued. "There's the parish church up near *The Farrier*, near Crowford Rise, and there's St. Andrews opposite Crowford Green, and there are at least three more than I don't even know the names of. There must be a priest or a vicar who'd want to help us." He paused for a moment, trying to think of some other options. "Or we could go to the town hall," he suggested, "or to Crowford Museum, or there are those people who complained about the church behind here getting knocked down, so we could try to get in touch with them. Someone has to be interested in putting this right."

"Do they?" Sasha asked. "I think you're putting too much faith in human decency."

"People are fundamentally good," he countered, "and I'm going to prove that by finding someone in the morning who'll help us sort all of this out."

He turned and looked down the staircase again.

"Lisa?" he called out. "We've been talking, and it looks like we probably won't be able to get the cops to help. We're going to have to wait until the morning, and then Crowford Museum's probably our best bet."

He waited for an answer.

"Lisa?"

"When did you become so naive?" Sasha muttered. "Listen, I've done what I can, but I think I might get out of here soon. I'd still like to track Derek down before all the pubs have shut, and it's obvious that we can't do much here."

"Sure, whatever," Josh replied, still looking down the staircase.

"Adios, you two," Sasha continued as she headed to the front door. "I've got to admit, this has been a blast, even if it's not something I'd wanna do every night." She pulled the door open and hesitated for a few seconds, before turning to look back at Josh. "Tomorrow we totally need to start getting people involved, so we can figure out what to do about this whole ghost situation. The bastard pushed me down the stairs next door and damn near killed me, so this thing is personal. You're working here tomorrow, right?"

"Right," Josh said absent-mindedly. "Lisa, are you okay down there?"

"I'll pop by," Sasha replied, before making her way outside and letting the door swing shut. "Don't forget to lock up!"

"Lisa, can you hear me?" Josh asked, having barely even noticed that Sasha was gone. He hesitated, and then he started making his way down the steps. "Lisa, we've completely drawn a blank, it's pretty obvious that no-one's gonna help us. I think Sasha's right, we need to wait until the morning and then figure out exactly who we can turn to. It's not like -"

Stopping suddenly, he saw to his horror that Lisa was down in the coffin, with the skeletal figure holding her tight and clamping one rotten hand across her mouth. Even as she struggled, Lisa seemed to be unable to break free, and a moment later several large cracks began to spread from the grave, ripping through the concrete floor and causing the walls to shudder.

"Lisa!" Josh shouted, racing forward. "Don't -"

Before he could finish, a large part of the ceiling crashed down, landing on him and knocking him to the ground. Coughing frantically as dust filled the air, he threw chunks of tile and plaster away and tried again to get to Lisa, but now the entire building was rumbling and seconds later another part of the ceiling fell on top of him; as wires and cables dropped into the darkness, Josh found himself pushed back until he was almost at the staircase. He could hear Lisa frantically trying to cry out, but he could no longer see her as more and more debris began to rain down from above.

"Lisa!" he yelled, trying to find a way to get to her, only for the rest of the ceiling to smash down and block his path. "Can you hear me? I'm going to get to you, okay? Just hold on for one minute and I'm going to get you out of there!"

He tried again to rush forward, but a huge chunk of the ceiling crashed down, smacking the side of his head and sending him falling back against the steps. Powerless to help, he could only watch now as the rest of the ceiling collapsed into the basement, and now the thunderous roar of so much damage was too loud even for Lisa's cries to break through.

"Lisa!" he shouted frantically, as dust began

to fill his eyes and nose, forcing him back even further. "Hold on! Lisa, I'm coming!"

CHAPTER TWENTY-NINE

COUGHING FRANTICALLY, TRYING TO bring up huge clumps of dust that had settled in the back of his throat, Josh stumbled out through the coffee shop's front door and dropped to his knees. He took a series of deep breaths, soaking in the fresh night air, and then he turned to see that carnage inside the shop.

Almost the entire floor had collapsed now, crashing down into a hole where the basement had been. Hugh clouds of dust filled the shop, and most of the chairs and tables had tumbled into the void below. Even the main counter, where Josh had stood for so many years and served coffee to the great and good of Crowford, was now on its side in what remained of the basement, surrounded by a mass of twisted metal and smashed brickwork. A moment later the upper sections of the building let out an ominous groaning sound, as if the whole place was about to collapse.

"Lisa!" Josh shouted desperately, even though he knew there was little chance she could ever find a way out. With tears in his eyes he pulled the door back open, but he had to step back almost immediately as fresh dust began to burst out from inside the store. "Lisa, can you hear me?"

Holding the front of his t-shirt up to cover his mouth and nose, Josh tried once again to step back into the shop. He was still coughing, though a little less frantically as he tried to wave away as much of the dust cloud as possible.

"Lisa!" he yelled. "If you can hear me, say something!"

The rumbling sound had stopped now, and the dust was starting to settle, revealing the full extent of the devastation. Almost nothing was left of Al's, and Josh could see now that a huge pile of debris was now filling the basement; anyone who'd been trapped down there would certainly be dead now, and even as he opened his mouth to call out he realized that Lisa couldn't possibly have survived. A moment later, as if finally shaken into action, the shop's burglar alarm began to blare, ringing out through the night and filling the High Street. For Josh, however, this sound seemed almost to be a million miles away; he could only stare at the scene of utter devastation and think back to the last time he'd seen Lisa.

"I'm sorry," he stammered, barely able to believe what had happened. "I tried... I mean, I tried to..."

His voice trailed off.

"I tried to save you," he added finally. "I didn't know that thing would... I mean, I didn't even know that it *could*, I just..."

Getting to his feet, he took a couple of steps back, but a moment later he turned as he heard footsteps racing closer along the street. Before he had a chance to react, Sasha slammed into him and then stopped to look into the ruins of the coffee shop.

"What the -"

Clearly lost for words, she stared at what had once been the floor.

"Where's Lisa?" she asked. "I heard a crashing sound and came back, but... Josh, where's Lisa? Did she go to get help?"

"She didn't make it out," he whispered.

"What do you mean?" she hissed, turning to him and grabbing him by the shoulders, shaking him hard. "Josh, you're not making sense! Talk to me! Where's Lisa?"

"She's in there!" he yelled, pointing at the shop as tears filled his eyes. "The ghost of Jacob Stadwyck, or the corpse of him or whatever you want to call it, pulled her into the coffin and then more cracks appeared on the floor, and then everything just collapsed. I tried to save her, I did everything I could, but I just couldn't get to her." He paused for a moment as they both stared at the door, and at the mess inside the shop. "He took her," he added finally. "Jacob Stadwyck dragged her down to join him in the grave."

***

For a couple of minutes Josh and Sasha could only stare in horror at the scene. They each wanted to say something to make everything seem better, but as the burglar alarm continued to ring out they remained silent. Help would eventually arrive, they knew that much, yet nobody could save Lisa. She was lost.

And then, hearing a scratching sound, Josh looked over his shoulder. At first he saw only the birthday card shop and the TV rental place opposite, but a moment later he looked down at the ground as he realized that the sound was coming from a manhole cover. A few seconds after that he saw that the cover was starting to move, before finally it lifted up and a hand reached up to grab the side.

"Help me!" Lisa gasped. "Anyone!"

"Lisa?" Josh stammered, barely able to believe what he was seeing.

"Is that you?" Sasha asked.

"Help me!" Lisa hissed. "Don't just stand there!"

"Right!" Josh said, as he and Sasha hurried over and began to help her out. "What are you doing down there?"

"The coffin collapsed into one of the old tunnels," she gasped, barely able to get any words out as she dragged what remained of Jacob Stadwyck's rotten body out from the depths. "You know the old smuggling tunnels that everyone talks about? Well, one runs right under the shop, and then I managed to find my way here." She hauled Jacob's corpse over the edge and threw it down against the pavement. "I don't mind telling you," she added, as she wiped her hands on her shirt, "that it's dark down there, and it stinks, and I think there are rats. Lots of rats."

"You should have left this bastard there," Sasha sneered, staring at Jacob's dead body.

"No way," Lisa replied, getting to her feet as Josh reached out to try to help her keep steady. "Leaving him underground is part of what allowed all this to happen in the first place. We're not gonna make the same mistake as all those other people in the past."

"Wait, is this still not over?" Sasha asked. "For real? What else is there left for us to do?"

"We have to finish this," Lisa said firmly,

staring down at the dead body on the pavement, "once and for all. Tonight. We have to destroy everything that's left of Jacob Stadwyck in a way that means he can't ever come back again."

"How do we do that?" Sasha replied. "With axes and hammers? Please tell me it's with axes and hammers."

"That's part of it," Lisa murmured, still watching the bones, "but just give him a few seconds. There's a little more to it than that. While I was down there, I came up with a plan, but we have to do something that no-one else who's encountered this ghost has ever done before. They all ran, they all panicked, and instead we're going to hold our nerve. Plus, we don't have axes or hammers, so we'll have to make do."

"Hold our nerve?" Sasha said, staring at the corpse for a few more seconds before turning to her. "What exactly does that mean? Why are you getting all cryptic on me?"

"Because I don't like what we're going to have to do," Lisa told her. "In fact, I hate it. You see, Jacob's ghost can reach out and possess living people. When he's not doing that, his ghost is back in his own body. That's it, that's his two states. We could kill the person he's possessing, but he'd just go back into his corpse. And we could smash the corpse, but he'd just leap out and take someone over."

She fell silent for a moment, as they both heard sirens in the distance, rising over the sound of the coffee shop's burglar alarm.

"So what are you suggesting?" Sasha asked. "How exactly do we do this? I'm all ears and I want to help, but if you've got a plan, you're gonna need to spell it out a little more clearly."

"Isn't it obvious?" she replied, before slowly turning to see that Josh was sitting by himself on a bench in front of the coffee shop.

"No," Sasha said, as she too turned to look at Josh, "it's not obvious. In fact, absolutely nothing about this entire situation is even remotely obvious. I would love if things were obvious, but they just aren't." She paused for a moment. "What about you, Josh?" she continued. "Is it obvious to you? Do you have any idea what the hell she's going on about?"

She waited, but Josh was merely sitting with his head bowed.

"What's up with you?" Sasha asked, before turning to Lisa again. "What's up with him? Has he got stitch or something?"

"That's not him," Lisa murmured, watching as Josh slowly looked up at them both with a big, broad grin plastered across his face. "That's not Josh. Jacob Stadwyck's doing it again. He's reached out from his rotten old bones and he's possessing Josh. Can't you see it in his eyes?"

"Young lady," Josh replied darkly, as sirens

raced closer and closer, "you strike me as being perhaps rather comely." He paused, before getting to his feet and taking a step forward. "All those other girls were so vacuous and immature, but you... I think you are going to make me the perfect wife."

CHAPTER THIRTY

"IS THIS PART OF the plan?" Sasha asked, staring at Josh with a horrified expression for a moment before turning to Lisa. "Huh? Please, Lisa, tell me this is part of the plan."

"The others were all so ungrateful," Josh snarled, as Jacob spoke through his mouth. "Even Hannah failed to see that I was paying her the ultimate compliment. She struggled so hard down there in the cold dark soil, even when she should have realized that there was no point. I must admit, in the confines of the box, her endless screams began to be a little... grating."

"Okay, this is getting creepier by the second," Sasha said, before swallowing hard. "I fail to see how this can be part of *any* plan."

"Josh, I need you to listen to me," Lisa said

firmly. "I know you're in there and I know you can hear me, and this might come as a surprise but I... I believe in you."

She hesitated before taking a step forward.

"Don't get too close!" Sasha hissed.

"You're a good person," Lisa continued, keeping her eyes fixed on Josh's grinning face as he in turn took a step toward her. "Just as importantly, you're a strong person. Josh, you can push this ghost out of your body. You might not realize that you can, but it's possible if you just focus really hard on my voice. You don't want to let him win, do you? Do you really want to let him use you like this? Do you really want to let him use your darkest desires?"

"He's making me feel really wrong," Sasha explained, taking a couple more steps back. "I don't think we should let him anywhere near us."

"After so many false starts," Josh said, taking another step toward her and reaching out a hand, "I see now that *you*, my dear, are the fairest of them all. You're the one who's going to show me the necessary gratitude. By welcoming you into my world, I'm extending to you a great honor. I ask only that you recognize that honor and seek to... pay me back in some way."

"Josh, push past him," Lisa said firmly, refusing to budge as he edged ever closer. "Do you see me running? No, because I'm going to stand firm, and the reason I'm going to stand firm is that I know you're a good guy, and I have absolute faith that you're going to be able to do this. Walter Stryke couldn't, and perhaps there are others who couldn't as well, but you absolutely have what it takes."

She paused, before stepping closer to Jacob Stadwyck's corpse as it lay on the ground.

"I've never really had faith in anyone before," she continued, forcing a smile as tears began to fill her eyes. "That's funny, huh? I've never really believed in someone, not like this. But I know you, Josh, and despite everything that's happened I'm certain that you're a really, truly good person."

"Laying it on a bit thick, aren't you?" Sasha whispered.

"Jacob Stadwych doesn't belong in your body," Lisa explained, keeping her eyes fixed on Josh. "The thoughts and feelings he's making you feel don't belong in your body either. This isn't the kind of person you're going to be. So many others have suffered at Jacob's hands, but eventually someone has to have the strength to push him out forever." She looked down briefly at the corpse again, and then back at Josh's face. "You remember me, Josh, don't you? And I know you can hear me. Look into my eyes and try to remember the good side of your personality. Try to remember who you really are."

"Such a pretty young thing," he replied with

a faint grin, before reaching out and touching the side of her face. She flinched, but she made no move to pull away. "You're going to make me the most wonderful wife. I do so like your... young flesh."

"Josh, fight him," she said through gritted teeth, hating the touch of his fingertips on her cheek.

"And we're going to be together forever," Josh's mouth added, before leaning closer to kiss her on the lips. "And ever. And ever. And -"

At the last second, before their lips could touch, he let out a gasp and his eyes opened wide.

"Lisa?" he stammered. "What -"

"Now!" she hissed, slamming her foot down against Jacob Stadwyck's skull, shattering the bone and then quickly kicking it again and again as Josh stumbled back. "Sasha, help me!"

"What do I do?" Sasha asked, hurrying over.

"Destroy it!" Lisa replied, already kicking the chest section. "Hurry, before it can defend itself!" As those words left her lips, she saw one skeletal arm reaching up, but she quickly kicked that too, shattering the bone. "Don't let him fight back!"

"This is for pushing me down the stairs!" Sasha said firmly, as she smashed the heel of her boot against what remained of Jacob's face. "You have no idea how much that hurt!"

***

"My coffee shop," Al said around one hour later, standing in the High Street and staring in at the ruined seating area, seeing only the pit where the floor had collapsed into the basement. "It's gone!"

Nearby, Josh was sitting shivering as several police officers made their way past. Lisa and Sasha were sitting either side of him, and after a moment Lisa reached over and put an arm around him.

"It's okay," she said finally. "It's over. Like... *properly* over this time."

"How can you be so sure?" Josh asked.

"Because I made sure of it," she told him. "I couldn't do anything to him while he was in your body, I just couldn't risk hurting you. And when he was in his own corpse, he was able to defend himself. So I knew my only bet was to destroy his bones as soon as he left your body. That way there was nothing for him to possess. His own body was dust, and you'd kicked him out."

"So where is he now?" Sasha queried. "I can't believe I'm even asking this question with a straight face, but... where did the ghost go?"

"Your guess is as good as mine," Lisa said, as a gentle breeze blew along the street. "I reckon now he doesn't have a body, he'll have a much harder time remaining cohesive. If you ask me, he'll just drift for a while and then fade to nothing. All he has to hold himself together is hatred and jealousy and greed, and I doubt any of that will last for too long. Hopefully now he can leave everyone alone." She paused for a moment. "There was so much anger contained in his soul," she added cautiously. "It's time to let that dissipate."

Before he could answer, Josh spotted two figures watching from the shadows. He opened his mouth to call out to Dorothy Maitland and Walter Stryke, but in that moment he was struck by a sense of peace on their faces, and a few seconds later they faded from sight, disappearing into the night air.

"You know," he said cautiously, "I think you just might be onto something."

Hearing voices, he looked the other way and saw to his surprise that Angela Grace was picking her way past the police cars. An officer lifted a line of tape so that she could pass; she glanced briefly at Josh, offering him a somewhat flat stare, before heading over to talk to Al.

"I wouldn't be surprised if she owns the building," Sasha murmured. "They say the Graces used to own half of Crowford, and I bet they've still got their hooks in a few parts of it."

"Come on, you three," one of the police officers said, gesturing for them to make their way over. "We need statements from you, and you might want to consider telling the truth this time. You can't seriously expect anyone to believe all that nonsense about ghosts and skeletons. I know my inspector's sympathetic to some of that rot, but most of us know when we're being lied to."

"Let's get this over with," Josh said, wincing as he got to his feet and began to make his way over with Sasha just a few feet behind. "Then I want to go home and just sleep for a month."

Lisa began to follow him, but at the last moment she heard the payphone nearby starting to ring. She looked around and saw that no-one else seemed bothered, so she stepped over to the phone and lifted the receiver, hesitating for a few seconds before putting it close to her ear.

Close, but not quite touching.

"Hello?" she said cautiously. "Who's there?"

"Help me," Jacob Stadwych's voice gasped, barely strong enough to leave the speaker. "I don't know... I can't... you must help me!"

"So you *did* find something else to possess after Josh pushed you out," Lisa replied as a shiver passed through her chest. "And after your body was destroyed. You couldn't just fade away, could you? You were determined to persist, even if that meant possessing an inanimate object."

"Help me," he said again. "I'm begging you. Don't leave me in this... this thing, whatever it is."

"Sorry," she said firmly, "but I really don't want to risk you escaping again."

With that she yanked the bottom of the cord, pulling it out of the box so that the receiver no longer functioned. She placed the broken receiver back in the cradle, and then – as Al continued to talk to Angela Grace, and as the lights of police cars flashed blue all around – she made her way over to join the others.

EPILOGUE

Several months later...

"OKAY," TIM SCOTT SAID, checking his watch as the students began to pack their things away, "that's the end of today's class, but make sure you get those homework assignments done for next week. We're going to be going over them in class, so there's really no point in turning up without anything to talk about, is there?"

As his fellow students prepared to leave, Josh took a little more time. He'd enjoyed the class and his mind was full of ideas for the assignment, but he still couldn't shake a slight sense of melancholy. Getting to his feet, he took his time putting his notebook into his backpack, and by the time he was ready to leave all the other students had already made their escapes from the classroom. Even Tim, the course's head lecturer, had scurried away into his office, leaving Josh all alone in the room.

The rustling of his backpack somehow seemed louder now, as if to emphasize the fact that nobody else was around.

Once he was done, he hauled the backpack over his shoulder and made his way out of the room. He had a few things to do in town before catching the bus home, and he needed to drop by the nursing home on the way and see his grandmother. She'd been settling in well, and the constant round-the-clock care seemed to be suiting her well. Angela Grace had very kindly offered to pay the bills, and she'd helped Josh out with his tuition fees as well; although he hadn't explicitly asked Angela what she wanted in return for all that assistance, he understood that she wanted him to keep his mouth shut about everything that had happened at the coffee shop and the supermarket, and in all honesty he was quite happy with that arrangement.

He headed away from the classroom, along the corridor and then out into the yard, while running through a mental checklist of everything he needed to do on his way to the bus station.

"Josh?"

Startled, he turned to see a few girls sitting

on a bench. One of the girls got to her feet and made her way over, but it still took Josh a couple of seconds before he recognized Lisa.

"Wow," he said, "you look... different."

"So do you," she replied cautiously. "It's... been a while."

"I didn't know you were studying here too."

"Media and Film Studies," she told him. "You?"

"Graphics," he replied. "Advertising too."

"This is so crazy," she continued with a nervous smile. "I hope you didn't think I was rude, not getting in touch after all that stuff that happened. After a few days, I just kind of wanted to forget all about it. I haven't really told anyone, either. To be honest, it barely even feels real now, it's almost like it was part of some kind of dream."

"Totally," he said, still shocked to see her at all.

"So are you still working at the coffee shop?" she asked.

"It's not reopening," he replied.

"Oh, right. Sorry, I moved out of Crowford a while ago and I haven't been back to visit."

"Al took the insurance money and moved on," Josh explained. "Now the coffee shop's just another in that long row of shuttered places. I know this might seem hard to believe, but somehow Crowford's gone even further downhill. I feel like, at this rate, there won't be much of a town left soon."

They stood in an awkward silence for a moment, neither of them really knowing what to say but both of them feeling as if they couldn't just walk away. Josh noticed that Lisa's friends were looking at him, and he began to worry that he might be blushing. At the same time, he was truly glad to see Lisa again and he hated the idea of just politely wishing her a good afternoon and walking away, even if – with each passing second – he felt as if he really had nothing more to say to her. Finally the anticipation grew too much and he realized that he should just leave her alone.

"I should get going," he said, turning to walk away. "The bus -"

"Do you want to get a drink?"

Shocked, he turned to her again and saw that a faint, nervous smile had reached her lips.

"A coffee or... tea?" she continued. "Like I said, all that stuff at the old coffee shop feels like a whole different lifetime. It's almost like we're not the same people, or at least... I guess we can start again. If we want. If *you* want. I mean, I'd like to. Start again, that is. Am I making sense, or am I just rambling?"

"No, you're making perfect sense," he replied, feeling a huge sense of relief. "You're making more sense than anyone's ever made in the history of the world."

"Let me just tell the girls that I won't be going to the cinema with them," she replied, and now it was her turn to blush a little. "Hey, at least we won't be short of anything to talk about, right?"

Left standing alone while Lisa talked to her friends, Josh found himself unable to quite believe that this was really happening. He'd thought of Lisa regularly since he'd last seen her, although he'd assumed that she was simply off being cool somewhere and that he'd never be lucky enough to bump into her again; he'd also figured that even in the unlikely event that they ever met, she'd have no interest in actually hanging out with him. Now, however, he watched as she made her way over to him, and together they began to make their way across the yard, heading away from the college.

"So that was pretty crazy a few months ago, right?" Lisa said with a smile. "Can you believe that ghosts actually ended up haunting a coffee shop, a shoe store and a supermarket?"

"That's nothing," Josh replied, already feeling at ease with her. "Did you ever hear the rumor about the old payphone in the High Street?"

BOOKS IN THIS SERIES

1. The Haunting of Nelson Street
2. The Revenge of the Mercy Belle
3. The Ghost of Crowford School
4. The Portrait of Sister Elsa
5. The Haunting of the Crowford Hoy
6. The Horror of the Crowford Empire
7. The Nightmare of Crowford Hospital
8. The Curse of the Crowford Grand
9. The Ghosts of Crossley Manor
10. The Siege of Crowford Castle
11. The Haunting of Crowford Station
12. The Graves of Crowford Rise
13. The Legend of the Crossley Stag
14. The Phantom of Crowford Theatre
15. The Terror of Crowford Carnival
16. The Secret of Adam Grey
17. The Haunting of Stryke Brothers

COMING SOON

18. The Ghost of Crowford Library

AMY CROSS

274

Also by Amy Cross

The Haunting of Nelson Street
(The Ghosts of Crowford book 1)

Crowford, a sleepy coastal town in the south of England, might seem like an oasis of calm and tranquility. Beneath the surface, however, dark secrets are waiting to claim fresh victims, and ghostly figures plot revenge.

Having finally decided to leave the hustle of London, Daisy and Richard Johnson buy two houses on Nelson Street, a picturesque street in the center of Crowford. One house is perfect and ready to move into, while the other is a fire-ravaged wreck that needs a lot of work. They figure they have plenty of time to work on the damaged house while Daisy recovers from a traumatic event.

Soon, they discover that the two houses share a common link to the past. Something awful once happened on Nelson Street, something that shook the town to its core.

AMY CROSS

Also by Amy Cross

The Revenge of the Mercy Belle
(The Ghosts of Crowford book 2)

The year is 1950, and a great tragedy has struck the town of Crowford. Three local men have been killed in a storm, after their fishing boat the Mercy Belle sank. A mysterious fourth man, however, was rescue. Nobody knows who he is, or what he was doing on the Mercy Belle... and the man has lost his memory.

Five years later, messages from the dead warn of impending doom for Crowford. The ghosts of the Mercy Belle's crew demand revenge, and the whole town is being punished. The fourth man still has no memory of his previous existence, but he's married now and living under the named Edward Smith. As Crowford's suffering continues, the locals begin to turn against him.

What really happened on the night the Mercy Belle sank? Did the fourth man cause the tragedy? And will Crowford survive if this man is not sent to meet his fate?

AMY CROSS

Also by Amy Cross

The Devil, the Witch and the Whore
(The Deal book 1)

"Leave the forest alone. Whatever's out there, just let it be. Don't make it angry."

When a horrific discovery is made at the edge of town, Sheriff James Kopperud realizes the answers he seeks might be waiting beyond in the vast forest. But everybody in the town of Deal knows that there's something out there in the forest, something that should never be disturbed. A deal was made long ago, a deal that was supposed to keep the town safe. And if he insists on investigating the murder of a local girl, James is going to have to break that deal and head out into the wilderness.

Meanwhile, James has no idea that his estranged daughter Ramsey has returned to town. Ramsey is running from something, and she thinks she can find safety in the vast tunnel system that runs beneath the forest. Before long, however, Ramsey finds herself coming face to face with creatures that hide in the shadows. One of these creatures is known as the devil, and another is known as the witch. They're both waiting for the whore to arrive, but for very different reasons. And soon Ramsey is offered a terrible deal, one that could save or destroy the entire town, and maybe even the world.

Also by Amy Cross

The Soul Auction

"I saw a woman on the beach. I watched her face a demon."

Thirty years after her mother's death, Alice Ashcroft is drawn back to the coastal English town of Curridge. Somebody in Curridge has been reviewing Alice's novels online, and in those reviews there have been tantalizing hints at a hidden truth. A truth that seems to be linked to her dead mother.

"Thirty years ago, there was a soul auction."

Once she reaches Curridge, Alice finds strange things happening all around her. Something attacks her car. A figure watches her on the beach at night. And when she tries to find the person who has been reviewing her books, she makes a horrific discovery.

What really happened to Alice's mother thirty years ago? Who was she talking to, just moments before dropping dead on the beach? What caused a huge rockfall that nearly tore a nearby cliff-face in half? And what sinister presence is lurking in the grounds of the local church?

Also by Amy Cross

Darper Danver: The Complete First Series

Five years ago, three friends went to a remote cabin in the woods and tried to contact the spirit of a long-dead soldier. They thought they could control whatever happened next. They were wrong...

Newly released from prison, Cassie Briggs returns to Fort Powell, determined to get her life back on track. Soon, however, she begins to suspect that an ancient evil still lurks in the nearby cabin. Was the mysterious Darper Danver really destroyed all those years ago, or does her spirit still linger, waiting for a chance to return?

As Cassie and her ex-boyfriend Fisher are finally forced to face the truth about what happened in the cabin, they realize that Darper isn't ready to let go of their lives just yet. Meanwhile, a vengeful woman plots revenge for her brother's murder, and a New York ghost writer arrives in town to uncover the truth. Before long, strange carvings begin to appear around town and blood starts to flow once again.

AMY CROSS

Also by Amy Cross

Haunted

Twenty years ago, the ghost of a dead little girl drove
Sheriff Michael Blaine to his death.

Now, that same ghost is coming for his daughter.

Returning to the small town where she grew up, Alex
Roberts is determined to live a normal, quiet life. For the
residents of Railham, however, she's an unwelcome
reminder of the town's darkest hour.

Twenty years ago, nine-year-old Mo Garvey was found
brutally murdered in a nearby forest. Everyone thinks
that Alex's father was responsible, but if the killer was
brought to justice, why is the ghost of Mo Garvey still
after revenge?

And how far will the real killer go to protect his secret,
when Alex starts getting closer to the truth?

Haunted is a horror novel about a woman who has to
face her past, about a town that would rather forget, and
about a little girl who refuses to let death stand in her
way.

AMY CROSS

AMY CROSS

AMY CROSS

AMY CROSS

Also by Amy Cross

Asylum
(The Asylum Trilogy book 1)

"No-one ever leaves Lakehurst. The staff, the patients, the ghosts... Once you're here, you're stuck forever."

After shooting her little brother dead, Annie Radford is sent to Lakehurst psychiatric hospital for assessment. Hearing voices in her head, Annie is forced to undergo experimental new treatments devised by a mysterious old man who lives in the hospital's attic. It soon becomes clear that the hospital's staff, led by the vicious Nurse Winter, are hiding something horrific at Lakehurst.

As Annie struggles to survive the hospital, she learns more about Nurse Winter's own story. Once a promising young medical student, Kirsten Winter also heard voices in her head. Voices that traveled a long way to reach her. Voices that have a plan of their own. Voices that will stop at nothing to get what they want.

What kind of signals are being transmitted from the basement of the hospital? Who is the old man in the attic? Why are living human brains kept in jars? And what is the dark secret that lurks at the heart of the hospital?

AMY CROSS

BOOKS BY AMY CROSS

AMY CROSS

AMY CROSS

For more information, visit:

www.amycross.com

Printed in Great Britain
by Amazon